She struggled  out her memo...

Only it didn't work. The aggressive gleam in her eyes challenged him.

Jake's hand settled impatiently on her spine, tipping her backward. His mouth parted hers with a hot, hard urgency that sent sensations coursing through her in a wild primitive response. Suddenly her arms were closing around him in collusion and acceptance.

The old mantel clock suddenly wheezed and rang out. Instantly both of them froze. Jake's breathing was thick and fast as he studied her with smoldering eyes.

Kitty gave herself a faint shake. "The line you're looking for is 'God, what have I done?'" Never had Kitty's ready tongue come more welcomely to her rescue than in that intense lacerating silence.

"Why the hell did you have to come back?" Jake demanded.

LYNNE GRAHAM was born in Ireland and, at the age of fifteen, submitted her first romantic novel, unsuccessfully. Just when she was planning a career, a Christmas visit home resulted in her having to make a choice between career or marriage to a man she had loved since her teens. They live in Ireland in a household overflowing with dogs, plants and books. When their daughter was a toddler, Lynne began writing again, this time with success.

Books by Lynne Graham

HARLEQUIN PRESENTS
1167—THE VERANCHETTI MARRIAGE
1313—AN ARABIAN COURTSHIP

Don't miss any of our special offers. Write to us at the following address for information on our newest releases.

Harlequin Reader Service
P.O. Box 1397, Buffalo, NY 14240
Canadian address: P.O. Box 603,
Fort Erie, Ont. L2A 5X3

LYNNE GRAHAM

an insatiable passion

Harlequin Books

TORONTO • NEW YORK • LONDON
AMSTERDAM • PARIS • SYDNEY • HAMBURG
STOCKHOLM • ATHENS • TOKYO • MILAN

Harlequin Presents first edition November 1991
ISBN 0-373-11409-5

Original hardcover edition published in 1990
by Mills & Boon Limited

AN INSATIABLE PASSION

CHAPTER ONE

'DON'T I know your face from somewhere?' The teenager in the shop stared fixedly at her.

She dug her change into her purse. 'I doubt it.'

Suddenly he laughed, his puzzled frown vanishing. 'I know what it is. You look like that actress, Kitty Colgan. You know the one—she plays Heaven in *The Rothmans*. My mum's glued to the TV every week.' He groaned, lifting the box of groceries off the counter before she could reach for it. 'She takes those soaps so seriously, she's really upset that Heaven's being killed off.'

'Let me take that,' she interposed. 'It's not heavy.'

'Heavy enough for a lady your size.' From his lanky height he grinned down at her with the unabashed friendliness of a spaniel puppy. 'I bet you get taken for Kitty Colgan regularly,' he teased.

She pulled open the door. 'No, this is the first time.'

'I suppose she'd be driving a Merc,' he mocked cheerfully as she unlocked the boot of the elderly, mud-spattered Ford parked outside. 'Well, you wouldn't want to be in her shoes right now anyway. She's lost her job and that film star she was shacked up with has found someone else. If she's got a Merc, she's probably going to have to trade it in for a more modest set of wheels!'

'Thanks.' She slammed down the boot-lid one second after he removed his fingers from danger.

'Are you staying somewhere round here?'

She settled back behind the wheel. 'Just passing through.'

'I wish I was,' he grumbled, staring down the quiet country road.

As Kitty drove off, she was trembling. So much for the disguise! Tugging off the wool cloche, she slung it in the back seat and ran manicured fingertips jerkily through the silver-blonde, waterfall-straight hair that had tumbled down to her slim shoulders.

Her strained violet-blue eyes accidentally fell on the small decorative urn and the bunch of white roses on the passenger seat. Instantly she looked away again but the damage was done. The gremlins in her conscience wouldn't leave her alone. She was coming home after eight years of exile... and she was arriving too late. All the wishing in the world wouldn't change that fact.

Four incredibly short days ago she had been happy, blissfully unaware of what lay ahead. On the flight from Los Angeles, all that had been on her mind were the gloriously empty weeks stretching before her and the plot of the thriller she had long been anxious to sit down and actually try to write. Within an hour of entering the London town house, her mood of sunny anticipation had been shattered.

As an appetiser to his ambitious plans for her next career move, Grant had imparted the news of her grand-mother's death—one month too late for her to attend the funeral.

'She died in her sleep,' he had volunteered drily. 'You weren't deprived of a death-bed reconciliation.'

He had deliberately withheld the information from her. If she had walked off the set of *The Rothmans* to fly back to England, she would have held up the production schedule on her last show. Nor might she have been free to take advantage of the part Grant had lined up for her in his latest film. But then that hadn't been the only reason why he had kept quiet about Martha Colgan's death. And somehow it was those other unspoken and even less presentable reasons which had contributed to her bitter attack on him and the subsequent violence of the argument which had followed.

They had both said things which would have been better unsaid. Censure rarely came Grant's way. He was an internationally acclaimed star of twenty years' solid standing. Humility wasn't his strong point. When crossed he had the malice of a toddler throwing a temper tantrum. But the split between them had been coming for a long time, Kitty acknowledged unhappily.

Neither of them had known that his valet had had his ear to the door. Or that the same man had been snooping and prying for months behind their backs so that he could make his fortune selling lurid revelations of their life together to one of the murkier tabloids. What he had overheard that afternoon had been juicy enough to send him out from cover to the nearest phone.

The story of their break-up had made headlines the next day. The night before she had unwittingly lent credence to the tale by leaving the town house in disgust to check into a hotel. Yesterday, Grant had flown out to the South of France with his arm round his glamorous co-star, Yolanda Simons. The sensationalised instalments in the newspaper had run for three agonising days.

None of it would bother Grant. With the single exception of the leak about his chin tuck last year, Grant saw all publicity as good publicity and he didn't think of a woman's reputation as a fragile thing. In all likelihood he would be laughing over the fact that, despite the household spy, the probing searchlight of the Press hadn't even come close to digging up the biggest secret of all.

But the recent media coverage had appalled Kitty. It had finally brought home to her that she had lived a lie for too long and she was now reaping the benefits of that notoriety.

Her car ate up the miles, steadily taking her deeper into the familiar windswept desolation of the moors. By twelve, sunlight was banishing the overcast clouds, dispelling all gloom from the rugged landscape, but the closer Kitty got to her destination, the more tense she became.

Two unalterable realities had shadowed her childhood. One was that her mother had died the day she was born, the other that Jenny Colgan hadn't been married. Kitty's grandparents had raised her solely out of a sense of duty, and love had played small part in her upbringing. A lonely child, she had been ignored at home and had found it difficult to mix with the other children in the village school.

No matter how hard she tried to shut them out, the memories were flooding back—memories inextricably interwoven with the haunting image of a man's darkly handsome features. Jake...Jake! Angrily she crushed back her over-sensitivity. But Jake Tarrant had preoccupied her every waking thought for more adolescent years than she cared to recall.

Her grandparents had been the poorest tenants on the Tarrant estate, her grandfather an embittered, antisocial man who blamed the landlord and his neighbours for his own inefficient farming methods. Kitty had first met Jake when she was five. She had been hiding behind a hedge watching him ride. A lordly, lanky and intimidating ten-year-old, he had trailed her home, assuming that she was lost and that someone would be looking for her.

In those days, Jake had boarded during the week at an exclusive public school, coming home at weekends and holidays to be left very much to his own devices. After the fright he had given her at their first meeting, it had taken him months to persuade her to come willingly close again.

He had bribed her into giving him her trust with sweets set down at strategic distances in her favourite haunts. She had had the shy, distrustful wildness of an animal, unused to either attention or company. Years later he had confessed that he had once tried the same routine with a fox. Well, he had failed to tame the fox, but he hadn't failed with Kitty.

Starved as she was of affection, Jake had won her ardent devotion with ease. He had brought her out of her shell and school had become far less of an ordeal. Jake had improved her poor grasp of grammar. Jake had helped her to read. She had trailed in his wake with jam jars when he had gone fishing, tagged at his heels when he had gone exploring, a sounding-board for Jake's ideas and ambitions. A scraggy little thing she'd been, all eyes and lank, long hair in jumble-sale clothes.

Loving Jake had come as naturally as breathing to her. She couldn't even remember when the child's blind adoration had become something much deeper, something so powerful that it had hurt sometimes just to look at him. It hadn't been a sudden infatuation. Then there hadn't been a time in her life when she could remember not loving Jake.

At an early age she had learnt the difference between them. She could still picture his mother looking at her with well-bred repulsion from the threshold of her elegant drawing-room.

'You can't bring that dirty little brat indoors, Jake. She can wait for you outside. Really, I do have to draw the line somewhere,' Sophie Tarrant had reproved shrilly.

Jessie, the Tarrant housekeeper, had given her a glass of milk on the back kitchen step. The lines of demarcation had been drawn then while she sat listening to Mrs Tarrant complaining to Jessie about her as if she were deaf.

'I don't know what he sees in the child...yes, I know, neglected. She's quite pathetic but I refuse to have her in the house. You know the family, Jessie. Very odd birds, I've been told. Take some of Merrill's outgrown clothes up to them. One does feel it's one's duty to do something.'

She had wanted to run away and sob her heart out, but she hadn't because she was waiting for Jake. Even then Jake had taken precedence over her self-respect. And even then Sophie Tarrant had been warning her off. When Kitty had reached sixteen, Jake's mother had cornered her one day and she had been even more blunt.

'You're developing the most ridiculous crush on Jake and, really, it won't do,' Sophie had scolded sharply, contemptuously. 'A childhood friendship is one thing, this pitiful infatuation of yours quite another. You are much too intense, Kitty, and I don't want to see you hurt. What I'm trying to tell you for your own good is that you don't move in the same social circles. You're being a very silly little girl. For goodness' sake, why don't you have a mother to tell you these things?'

Had she listened? Had she learnt? Not a bit of it. With the stubborn insouciance of extreme youth, she had clung to her love and her dreams. Who could ever have guessed that her worst enemy had given her sound and sage advice?

With a shudder of self-contempt, Kitty drew her straying mind back to the present. The Ford sped over the stone bridge into the village. Mirsby was a straggling clutch of terraced granite cottages and other buildings climbing a bleak hillside. She accelerated up the steep incline without looking either left or right. At the top she turned down the lane siding the weathered, unadorned bulk of the church and parked outside the cemetery.

The wind tore at her hair as she climbed out. In the biting cold she shivered. The Colgans were all buried in the oldest part of the graveyard. Kitty was the last Colgan and, ironically, the only one ever to own the land. When the Tarrant estate had been broken up and sold, her grandfather had travelled all the way to London to demand that she give him the money to buy the farm.

But his pride had insisted that the farm remain in her name.

One of the solicitor's letters, awaiting her in London, had contained an offer to buy Lower Ridge. The naturally sultry line of her mouth compressed with bitterness. She wouldn't sell. Year by year the buildings could crumble and the moors could inch back slowly over the fields. In her lifetime, Lower Ridge would never be Tarrant land again.

She arranged the roses in front of the plain gravestone. Her damp eyes stung in the breeze. After a moment's pause, she retraced her steps. The traditional gesture was all that she had to offer, all that either of her grandparents had ever wanted from her. Respect and obedience—nothing more, nothing less.

She didn't see the battered Land Rover sitting behind her car until she passed through the gate again. The storm-singed bulk of an ancient yew tree had hidden both it and the man propped up against the wall. There was no second of warning, no opportunity to avoid him.

He was very tall, very dark and very lean. Way back in the mists of time a Tarrant had reputedly stooped to marry a lady of gypsy origins and his forebears must have somersaulted inside their ancestral tombs. Jake Tarrant bore the stamp of that Romany heritage boldly against blonde, conventional siblings. His shaggily cut, overlong black hair framed a striking, sculpted bone-structure and dark mahogany eyes of animal direct intensity.

By any standards he was a sensationally attractive male. What made him exceptional was the almost brutal strength of character sheathed by formidable self-control that looked out of his hard stare. There was no trace of boyishness left in his features. The passions that had once run high enough to breach Jake's principles of honourable fair play were leashed now by maturity.

Her lightning-fast appraisal braced her reed-slender figure into defensive stillness. 'Surprise, surprise,' she managed, her beautiful face discomposed for only a split second.

It didn't show that her heart was pounding like a road drill and her stomach had cramped into sick knots. And that was all that mattered to Kitty. You didn't betray weakness to an enemy. Especially not if he had once put you on an emotional rack and cruelly stretched you until every sinew snapped. That was part of the Colgan code she prided herself on.

Fluidly straightening, he closed the distance between them. His hand reached out and covered the clenched fingers she held against her abdomen. In shock she surveyed that hand, that flesh touching hers in a movement of silently expressed sympathy. This same male had turned on her with derisive distaste six years earlier at her grandfather's funeral. Instinctively she stepped back, breaking the connection. Hatred that was a hard core of emotion inside her shot through her veins in an adrenalin boost that banished her exhaustion.

'I saw you driving through the village.' The well-bred, deep-pitched drawl was curiously clipped, lacking the measured resonance she recalled.

Kitty arched an imperious brow, several shades darker than her pale hair. 'So?' she challenged.

Guardedly he studied her. 'Was it my fault that you didn't attend her funeral?'

'Your fault?' she echoed with a brittle laugh. 'Still a Tarrant to the backbone, aren't you? You still have delusions about your own importance. I wasn't at the funeral, Jake, because I didn't know about it.'

He dug his lean hands deep into the pockets of his shabby, khaki jacket. 'I spoke to Maxwell on the phone within hours of her death. At the time I thought you were over in London. You'd been on a talk show.'

'It was pre-recorded.'

'I did attempt to contact you personally. Maxwell was extremely unhelpful,' he informed her with aggressive bite. 'But I still assumed he'd pass on the message.'

She shrugged. 'He did ... when it suited him. I didn't realise that it was you who had phoned. I suppose there was no one else,' she conceded. 'And I suppose it was a kindly thought, worthy of that well-known streak of Tarrant benevolence towards the less fortunately placed of the community——'

'I happened to be her closest neighbour,' he interrupted harshly.

'For what it's worth,' she trailed the word out, 'thanks.'

He planted a hand roughly against the pillar of the gate, imprisoning her between his long, powerful body and the wall. 'Look, I didn't follow you up here to play stooge to the smart-mouth lines!' he slung.

Delighted to have got a rise out of him, Kitty leant back sinuously against the pillar in taunting relaxation. 'Exactly why did you follow me up here?'

Shooting her a hard, driven glance, he swung restively away from her. 'All right, I owe you an apology for what I said at Nat's funeral.' His tone was abrasive, quite unapologetic.

She strolled away from the wall to stand at the thorn hedge boundary on the other side of the lane. The scent of him was still in her sensitive nostrils. He smelt of horses and soap and fresh air. Mentally she suppressed the unwelcome awareness. 'Is there anything else?' she enquired coldly. 'I have to call with Gran's solicitor.'

'I have the only set of keys for Lower Ridge.'

Her incredulous eyes flew to him. 'What are you doing with them?'

He looked steadily back at her. 'I've been keeping an eye on the place. Not by choice. Your grandmother made me executor of her will.'

Kitty vented a shaken laugh. 'Oh, really?'

'I didn't find out until then that you bought the farm for them. Where they got the money to buy it was a mystery round here for a long time afterwards.' He absorbed her shuttered, uninterested stare, and his nostrils flared. 'You know that I want to buy Lower Ridge. The offer is over the market price. Morgan personally checked that out before he passed it on to you.'

'He took a lot on himself without my instructions,' she noted cuttingly.

'You couldn't get away from that farm fast enough or far enough eight years ago,' he countered. 'I can't see what you'd want with it now.'

The wind blew the floating panels of her black Italian knit cape taut against the full swell of her breasts and the shapely curve of her hips. Stonily she looked at him. 'No, Rodeo Drive is much more my style. That's where I belong.' With bitter relish she threw his own words at her grandfather's funeral back in his teeth. 'What right had you to say that to me?'

'Maybe no right, but it was the truth,' he stated unflinchingly. 'What kind of a reception did you expect when you rolled up in your fancy limousine with a pack of reporters baying at your heels? You could have come up here quietly, but you didn't. You managed to turn a solemn occasion into a riotous publicity stunt.'

Fury spurred her into an emotional response. 'It was an accident. I didn't think!'

Meeting his cool, unimpressed gaze, she spun her head away and stared out blindly across the fells, but even with her back turned to him she could feel his disruptive presence as strongly as she could feel the rebellious breeze clawing at her hair.

'I'm afraid I haven't got the keys on me, but if you want them...' he murmured.

'I want them,' she said flatly.

'I'll go back to Torbeck and pick them up,' he completed.

'Good.' Without warning she turned her head back and intercepted the fierce glitter of gold in his un-screened gaze before he could conceal it. Countless men had looked at Kitty with acquisitive desire over the years. None of them had incited the smallest interest in her. But that instant of weakness on his part filled her with wild exhilaration. Eat your heart out, Jake, she urged inwardly; just look at what you threw away.

His dark skin was stretched taut over his hard bone-structure. 'My God, Kitty, we used to be friends,' he condemned in a scathing undertone.

'Past tense still operative,' she spelt out.

'Have you had lunch?' he asked abruptly, glancing fleetingly at his watch.

'No, but I suggest you go back to your wife for yours,' she responded, softly sibilant. 'That is where *you* belong.'

He stiffened. Antagonism sizzled in the air. Hot and seething.

'Liz is dead, Kitty. She died in a car crash almost two years ago.'

A pregnant pause ensued, unbroken by any conventional offer of sympathy. She surveyed him impassively, her ability to control her features absolute. Dead, she's dead. Kitty didn't want to think about that. She had never met Liz Tarrant. Liz had managed to live and die without ever finding out how much Kitty Colgan had once hated her for having what she had foolishly believed should have been hers. She had got over that mindless loathing. Why hate the faceless Liz? Jake had married her; Jake had let Kitty down. So he was a widower now, a one-parent family of x number of kids...so what?

In the silence impatience mastered him first. He drove long, supple fingers through the black hair falling over his brow. 'I'll meet you up at Lower Ridge in half an hour with the keys.'

She conveyed agreement with a mute nod, watched him spring up into the Land Rover, worn denim closely sheathing his long, straight legs to accentuate the well-honed muscularity of his lean, athletic build. He didn't need designer clothes to look good. An intensely masculine specimen, Jake was a compellingly handsome man. It galled her that she should still notice the fact.

When he was gone, she got into her car. Her hands were shaking. Weakly she rested her head back, her throat thick and full.

Her grandparents had insisted that she leave school at sixteen, but jobs had been hard to find locally. By then she had already been waiting table the odd evening at the Grange. Sophie had suggested it. Sophie had deliberately put Kitty in her social place for her son's benefit.

Jake had been at university and he had often brought friends home for the weekend. A new, disturbing dimension had gradually entered their once close friendship, throwing up barriers that hadn't existed before.

Jake had avoided her. When he had seen her, his reluctance to touch her had been pronounced. Abrupt silences would fall where once dialogue had been easy. A crazy heat that alternately frightened and excited her would electrify the air between them.

Correctly interpreting that sexual tension had made her misinterpret the strength of Jake's feelings. She had convinced herself that Jake was only waiting for her to grow up and that she didn't really have to worry about those sophisticated girls with their cut glass accents, who regularly appeared in the passenger seat of his sports car.

Looking back, she recoiled from her adolescent fantasies. She hadn't even had the social pedigree to qualify as an acceptable girlfriend. Jake had been uncomfortable with her menial employment in his home. He

hadn't said so, though. He had known her grandparents
had had a struggle to survive.

Had it been pity that brought him to her home that
Christmas Eve with a present for her? An enchanting
little silver bracelet, the first piece of jewellery she had
ever had. There had been a light in his dark tawny eyes
as he had given it to her, a light that had seemed to make
nonsense of his casual speech. Her heart had sung like
a dawn chorus while her grandfather had turned turkey-
red. Letting her accept the gift had practically choked
him.

Every New Year's Eve the Tarrants had held open
house for half the county. Jessie had persuaded Martha
Colgan that Kitty should sleep over at the Grange as it
would be a very late night.

Sophie Tarrant had been in a filthy mood that evening
when her husband had failed to put in an appearance.
She had continually phoned their London apartment and
her anger had split over into sharp attacks on the staff.
By then even Kitty had understood that for years Jake's
parents had lived virtually separate lives because of his
father's extra-marital affairs.

Shortly before midnight, a drunken guest had cornered
Kitty in the hall and tried to kiss her. Jake had yanked
him away, slamming him bruisingly back against the wall.
'Keep your hands off her!' he had snarled, scaring the
wits out of Kitty and her assailant with an unnecessary
degree of violence.

As the guest had slunk off, Jake had spun back to her
where she had stood pale and trembling in the shadows
of the stairwell. Just as suddenly he had reached for her,
his lean, still boyish body hard and hungry against hers,
his mouth blindly parting her lips. But she had barely
received the tang of the whisky on his breath before he
had pushed her away, a dark flush highlighting his
cheekbones. 'I'm not much better than that bastard I

just tore off you,' he had vented in self-disgust. 'You're still a kid.'

'I'm almost eighteen,' she had argued strickenly.

'You're six months off eighteen,' he had gritted, and when she had attempted instinctively to slide back into his arms his hands had clamped to her wrists. 'No!' he had snapped in a near savage undertone. 'And whose idea was it to bring you in here tonight? There are too many drunks about. You ought to be up in bed.'

Her vehement protests that every hand was needed had been ignored. Jake had been immovable. 'I haven't even had anything to eat yet,' she had complained in humiliated tears. 'I hope you're pleased with yourself.'

At some timless stage of the early hours, distant noises still signifying the ongoing party downstairs, Jake had shaken her awake and presented her with a heaped plate of food. It had begun as innocently as a children's midnight feast. She had sat up in bed eating while Jake had lounged on the foot of it, far from sober as he had mimicked some of his mother's most important guests with his irreverent ability to pick out what was most ridiculous about them.

A rapt audience, she had got out of bed to put the plate back on the tray. When she had clambered back they had been mysteriously closer. Had that been her doing? His? He had touched her cheek, his hand oddly unsteady.

'Kiss me,' she had whispered shyly.

'I'll kiss you goodnight,' he had breathed almost inaudibly. 'Oh, God, Kitty,' he had muttered raggedly into her hair on his passage to her readily parted lips. 'I love you.'

Overwhelmed by his roughened confession, Kitty had pressed herself to him and clung. That first kiss had gone further than either of them intended. For her there had been more pain than pleasure, but that hadn't mattered to her. Belonging to Jake had been a sufficient source of joy. She had naïvely believed that now there would be no need for him to date other girls. Her grasp of human interplay had been that basic. It had never occurred to her that she was simply satisfying an infinitely less high-flown need in Jake that night.

Only afterwards had she realised that Jake had been more drunk than he had been merely tipsy. She did remember him mumbling something along the lines of, 'God, what have I done?' in a dazed mix of shock and self-reproach.

Rousing herself shakily from her unwelcome recollections, Kitty started up her car, winding down the window to let cold air sting her pale cheeks. Both their lives had changed course irrevocably in the weeks that had followed.

Jake's father had died suddenly, leaving a string of debts. Jake had had to leave university, abandon his training as a veterinary surgeon. He had had no choice. His mother and his sisters had become his responsibility. In the end the estate had still been sold. A financial whiz-kid couldn't have saved it. She wondered vaguely where they all lived now. Torbeck, he had mentioned. That was a farm higher up the valley, no more than a mile from Lower Ridge across the fields. For the life of her, she couldn't imagine Jake's mother living in an ordinary farmhouse.

A rough, pot-holed track climbed steeply to Lower Ridge. A squat, stone-built cottage, backed by tumbledown outhouses came into view. The guttering sagged, the metal windows were badly rusted. In eight years she had not been welcome here. She stared at the cottage. It was lonely, sad. How had she ever believed that she could stay here to write her book? Her subconscious mind had somehow suppressed this unattractive reality.

'What is with this desire to make a pilgrimage back to your roots?' Grant had demanded furiously. 'They're better left buried and you certainly don't owe that woman a sentimental journey.'

With sudden resolution, Kitty walked back to her car. But before she could execute her cowardly retreat, a Range Rover came up the lane. Jake sprung out. Clay-coloured Levis and a rough tweed jacket worn with an open-necked shirt had replaced his earlier attire. He had changed his clothes as well as his vehicle.

Dear God, could he be serious about the lunch invitation? A civilised exchange of boring small talk? It seemed he wasn't quite averse to the legend of Kitty Colgan and the sex-symbol image Grant had worked so hard to create for her. If it hadn't been so tragic, it would have been hysterically funny.

When a man kissed Kitty, she could plan a grocery list in her head. Her provocative image was a make-believe illusion. She had all the promise on the outside and she couldn't deliver except for a camera. And here she was standing looking at the cruel bastard responsible for her inadequacy.

He unlocked the front door. 'It took me longer than I estimated,' he said wryly. 'I'd mislaid the keys in a safe place.'

Had he taken more than half an hour? She hadn't noticed. Time had lost its meaning for her outside the cemetery.

Tawny eyes met hers with merciless directness. 'Perhaps you'd prefer to be on your own. I don't want to butt in.'

'You're not butting in on anything but memories, and none of them worth the proverbial penny,' she quipped half under her breath, stilling an impulse to admit that she had lost her fancy to reacquaint herself with her former home.

The wind pushed the door back on its hinges. A steep staircase rose just a step away, the entrance the exact depth of the two doors that opened off it, one on either side.

Kitty pushed down the stiff handle on the parlour door. The three-piece suite was old as the hills but still new in appearance through rare use. It was a room rather pitifully set aside for the exclusive entertainment of guests in a tiny house where there had never been visitors.

She mounted the creaking stairs. The bathroom, put into the box-room when she was thirteen, was a slot above the scullery below. Time had been kind to the walls of her old room, fading the virulent green paint she had hated. The old bookcase was still crammed with childhood favourites, every one of which had originally belonged to a Tarrant child.

Steeling herself, she walked into her grandparents' room. It was the same. The high bed, the nylon quilt, cracked linoleum complaining beneath her stiletto heels. Jake stood silently behind her, yet she was overpoweringly aware of his proximity and she shied automatically away from his tall, well-built body to pass back down the stairs.

One room remained, the kitchen-cum-dining-room where the day-to-day living had gone on. Despising her over-sensitivity, she thrust open the door. Jake moved past her to open the curtains. Light streamed in over the worn tiles on the floor, picking out the shabbiness of the sparse furniture.

'I knew you'd come back,' he said curtly.

She lifted her chin, denying the tension holding her taut. 'Am I so predictable?' she asked sweetly.

He dealt her a hard glance. 'That wasn't the word I would have used.'

Colouring, she avoided his steady appraisal and forced a determined smile. 'Nothing here seems to have changed.'

His mouth twisted expressively. 'Did you think it would have? Did you think it was enough for you to play Lady Bountiful from a safe distance?'

'I don't know what you're talking about,' she lied.

Black lashes partly obscured his glinting downward scrutiny. 'Martha can only have cut you dead at Nat's funeral out of some misguided sense of loyalty to him,' he spelt out with cruel emphasis. 'I'm sure she regretted doing it.'

'She didn't.' Her contradiction was immediate.

'How would you know? You never came back again to find out!' he dismissed brusquely. 'Was your pride so great that in six years you couldn't give her a second chance?'

His biting criticism stabbed into her. No matter what story had been put about by her grandparents, Kitty had been shown the door and firmly told that she was never to return. But there was no point in making a defence that would encourage questions that she couldn't and wouldn't answer. Jake would want to know why they had done that.

'I didn't fancy being turned from the door and I would have been,' she said tightly. 'I wrote to her... I wrote I don't know how many times and she didn't reply to one of my letters. Her silence spoke for her. She always was a woman of few words.'

He frowned. 'You wrote to her?'

'Didn't the bush telegraph pick that up as well?'

'I really did believe that she might have felt differently from Nat.' His response lacked the acid sarcasm of hers.

Her eyes hardened. 'Don't talk about my grandparents as if you knew them. You never knew them on an equal footing. In their eyes you were always a Tarrant, a breed apart, what Gran used to call "our betters". I doubt you ever had a single real conversation with either of them.'

Anger had paled his complexion. 'You talk as though we're living in the nineteenth century.'

'But we did in this house.' And in yours, her skimming look of scorn implied.

Although it visibly went against the grain to abandon the argument on class divisions, his mouth remained firmly shut.

'I guess you'd like to know how I came to buy this place,' she continued offhandedly. 'Grandfather came to London and asked me to. He said it was the least of what I owed them.'

Jake quirked a black brow. 'Do you blame him for his attitude? You ran away and you disappeared into thin air. Almost two years later you popped up in print at a movie première with Maxwell...'

And it felt good, so good, she affixed inwardly. Diamonds at my throat and a designer gown, the stuff of which dreams are made. 'I imagine that set the natives back on their heels,' she mocked.

'Oh, yes, you were the sole topic of conversation locally for months,' he agreed tongue in cheek. 'Talk about rags to riches.'

She gave a little smile. 'I try not to. Other people find the Cinderella story terribly boring.'

'Are you casting Maxwell as the fairy godmother or the dashing young prince? Either way he made a pretty sordid match for a nineteen-year-old girl,' he drawled with a derisive softness that stung. 'And I still wouldn't have thought that you had the money to buy this farm at that early stage of your...career.'

Ignoring that insolent hesitation, she shrugged. 'I didn't. Grant bought it for me.' And it would knock you for six if you knew what else his representative bought at the same time, she thought with malicious amusement.

'How very generous of him.'

'He's extremely generous.' If anything irritated, inconvenienced or demanded, slap a cheque down hard on it. That was how Grant functioned. Unfortunately it usually worked for him. Back then it had worked with Kitty. She had confused generosity with caring. A bad mistake.

Jake's dark, unfathomable gaze rested on her, 'You treat me like an enemy.'

'Do I?' She produced a laugh worthy of applause. 'We're strangers now, Jake.'

He probed the bright smile that sparkled on her lips. 'I never meant to hurt you, Kitty.'

'Hurt me?' she prompted, tilting her head back enquiringly.

He swore in sudden exasperation. 'For God's sake, will you drop the Heaven Rothman act? Or has that nymphomaniac superbitch you've been playing for so long somehow become you?' he demanded crushingly. 'There are no microphones or cameras about. Do you think Kitty could come out of the closet for five minutes?'

CHAPTER TWO

'I ONLY perform for my friends, and you're not numbered among them.' Stormily Kitty flung her head back, a line of pink demarcating the exotic slant of her cheekbones. Bitter resentment shuddered through her, fighting to the surface in spite of her efforts to contain it. 'Since you came into this house your hypocrisy has amazed me! For a start, you didn't like my grandparents. And at least you had the guts to be honest about that eight years ago. You thought Nat had a chip the size of a boulder on his shoulder. You thought Martha was a sour, cold woman. And you were right...you were right on both counts!'

Jake stood there, effortlessly dominating the cramped confines of the room. Dark and controlled, he murmured, 'Martha mellowed a good deal after his death.'

'Not towards me, she didn't!'

'You're upset,' he drawled flatly. 'I'll leave. I shouldn't have stayed.'

Her hand sent the door crashing shut. 'No, you won't leave until I've had my say,' she declared shakily. 'Why have you decided to rewrite the past? I had the most miserable childhood here and you know it. Once in seventeen years my grandmother put her arms around me. She must have had to hold me to feed me when I was a baby, but I don't remember it. I remember being a burden, a nuisance and an embarrassment. My grandfather didn't get the chance to punish my mother, so he punished me instead...'

Her voice broke and she turned to the window, bracing her trembling hands on the dusty sill. 'I remember it all,' she muttered, forcing out the harshened syllables very low, 'as if it were yesterday.'

The profound silence stretched on and on.

'Why did you come up here?'

Numbly she fought to recapture her poise. 'I just wanted...to see it.'

'Well, now you've seen it...'

'Do you have children?' As soon as the question left her lips, she could have bitten her tongue out. That dangerous explosion of emotion had left her temporarily out of control.

'A little girl.' He hesitated. 'She's four years old.'

A sudden ache stirred in Kitty's breasts, violent, unforgiving. But his admission iced back over her seething emotions. Her voice emerged quietly and cleanly. 'If you don't mind, I would like to be on my own now.'

'No problem. I've got a lunch date to keep,' he said curtly.

Her arrogant assumption that he had intended to invite her gave her a sharp pang. Of course she wouldn't have gone. You didn't dive when you were bleeding into a river full of crocodiles. All the same, it would have been nice to have been asked so that she could have refused. 'Who is she?' she asked lightly.

At the door he paused, his dark scrutiny hooded. 'You wouldn't know her. She wasn't here in your time.'

'My goodness, but you're being coy, Jake,' she purred, and she was Heaven Rothman to her fingertips, poised, indulgently amused.

Long, supple fingers flexed against the door-frame. 'Her name's Paula. She's the nurse in the local practice.'

She smiled. 'What does she look like?'

A suffocating tension alive with hostile undertones had thickened the atmosphere. A muscle jerked at the corner of his wide, sensual mouth. 'Are you going to ask if I've slept with her as well?' he slung at her caustically.

He shocked her into silence. Her startled gaze fled his aggressive stare. She looked away from him. In the interim, he walked out of the house, slammed into his car and drove off. She breathed again. Pain was still stabbing through her and she didn't understand why. Two hours ago she had believed that Jake was married. Now she knew he was unmarried and involved. What was the difference? She couldn't possibly be jealous. The very idea was laughable after all these years.

With a sigh she slumped down into an armchair. Hunger was making her dizzy. Common sense told her that she was in no fit state to drive. She would bring in the groceries and make herself a sensible snack before she left to find a hotel as far from here as she could get by evening.

He hadn't said goodbye. But then they'd never said goodbye to each other. Ever. It seemed that habit remained. And without conscious volition Kitty was swept back to the aftermath of that night she had spent in his arms.

She had felt guilty, but she hadn't felt ashamed...then. Innocently trusting in that confession he had made, she had believed there was no cause for shame where there was love.

It had taken him twenty-four hours to seek her out— a Jake who was a complete stranger to her. A bitter despair and a distaste that had pierced her to the very centre of her being had shown nakedly in his shadowed eyes before he had looked away.

'What happened between us was very wrong. I wish to God I could wipe it out, but I can't.' His intonation had been low and precise, as if he had rehearsed the entire speech beforehand. 'Your grandparents trusted me and I've broken that trust. I've got no excuse. I'm five years older and wiser and I should never have touched you.'

'If you love me, it——'

'But that's just the point. I don't love you in the way a man loves a woman. I care for you deeply as a friend...as a kid sister, if you like,' he had forced out in harsh interruption.

'I love you,' she had whispered, not even able to absorb what he was telling her. It hadn't seemed real. Nightmares had that quality.

'It's an infatuation and it will die,' he had overruled fiercely. 'Last night was a mistake, Kitty. I was drunk. That doesn't excuse me, but that's the only reason it happened. It wasn't your fault, it was mine.' He had stopped to clear his throat. 'If there should be consequences...'

'Consequences?' she had repeated blankly.

'If you prove to be pregnant,' he had grated hoarsely, 'I'll stand by you, I'll deal with your grandparents. But I won't marry you. A marriage between us wouldn't work. The risk of pregnancy isn't that great, but if it should happen I promise you that I'll look after everything. However, the pregnancy will have to be terminated,' he had concluded harshly.

Three weeks later he had come to her with haunted eyes and gaunt cheekbones. 'Thank God,' he had muttered rawly, let off the hook.

He had married Liz quietly in London, the ceremony unattended by any of his family.

They said hearts didn't break. Kitty's had. The news of his marriage had shocked everybody, but it had devastated her. It was one thing to humbly accept that he didn't love her, another thing entirely to accept that he could love and marry someone else. She had lost so much more than a lover. He had been closer to her than her own family. He had been her only real friend. And he had dropped her like a hot potato, retreating with appalled speed from the trap he had seen opening up in front of him. For him that night really had been a disastrous mistake.

He could have let her down more gently. She was convinced Liz hadn't been in the background then. His own family had known nothing whatsoever about her. But what embittered Kitty most of all was his refusal to admit that he had ever wanted her. A man didn't make love to a female firmly fixed in his mind as an extra sister. Then, had he employed any other excuse, she might still have harboured hopes. And Jake had been determined to kill even her hopes stone-dead.

Other later memories intruded and she struggled fiercely to close them out...only it didn't work. She had lied to him when she had told him that she wasn't expecting his child. Of course she had lied. He had given her no other choice. And ironically, in the end, that lie hadn't made any difference. A few months later, she had had a miscarriage. Nature's way, the doctor had said bracingly. For a long time afterwards she had suspected that, had she enjoyed proper medical attention during those crucial early weeks of pregnancy, the outcome might have been very different. She had grieved deeply for that loss, but she had grieved alone.

Grant had said it was for the best, quite unable to understand how she could possibly have wanted the baby after Jake had married Liz. But she had wanted that baby. She had wanted that baby more than she had ever wanted anything either then or since. Slowly she sank back to the present, raising chilled hands to her tear-wet face. Without realising it, she drifted slowly into sleep.

It was pitch-dark when she awoke, freezing cold and stiff. Stumbling up on woozy legs, she fumbled for the light switch. No light came on. The scullery light was equally unresponsive.

'You idiot,' she muttered, realising what the problem was. The electricity was off. Indeed, she hadn't been thinking clearly when she had impulsively planned her stay here.

Luckily her grandmother had been a very methodical woman. The torch still hung above the fridge. Kitty's watch told her it was nearly ten. It was too late to drive off in search of a hotel. There was food in the car, probably coal or wood in the fuel shed, and she could bring a mattress downstairs to sleep by the fire. She emptied the car and then parked it in the barn out of sight.

With damp matches, she needed perseverance to light a fire. Once she had a promising glow in the grate, she lit the bottled gas cooker and put a now defrosted dish of lasagne into the oven. That done, she located candles in an upper cupboard and switched on the water below the sink. There she came unexpectedly on an unopened bottle of sherry.

By midnight she was sitting cross-legged on top of her makeshift bed, washing back her lasagne with a glass of sherry. Grant would have cringed in fastidious horror from the sight, she conceded ruefully. Already her anger with him was fading. Grant couldn't help being self-centred, possessive and manipulative.

Eight years ago she had hurled herself into Grant's arms in a London hotel suite. A frightened and lost teenager, she had been perilously close to a nervous breakdown. The responsibility must have horrified him, but Grant hadn't been the star of a dozen box-office hits on the strength of looks alone. He had hidden his feelings well. If Grant had rejected her, she would have thrown herself in the Thames. She had had too many rejections to bear one more.

His greatest pleasure had been the successful stage-management of her career. Grant loved to play God. He had made her over from outside in before sending her to drama school in New York. That first year had been a chaotic whirl of new experiences and some truly terrifying ordeals.

The fire was making her uncomfortably warm. Getting up, she removed a silk nightshirt from her case and undressed, ruefully wondering how long it would take her to get to sleep. Insomnia had been her most pressing problem of late. Ironically, it was also what was responsible for the short story she had written and had published in a magazine the previous year. She had sat up scribbling until exhaustion had taken its toll.

As she poured herself another sherry, she tried to concentrate on the intricate plot of the thriller she was planning. It shouldn't have been difficult. She had been dreaming about the book for months, impatient to sit down and write without distractions.

A faint noise jerked her head up from her notepad. Her eyes dilated, a stifled gasp of fear fleeing her lips. A large dark shape had filled the scullery doorway.

'I don't believe this.' Jake strode into the flickering shadows of mingled fire and candlelight. He towered over Kitty like a dark avenging angel. 'I could see the light from the road. I thought someone had broken in.'

Behind her breastbone, her heart was still involved in terrified palpitations. 'How did you get in? The doors are both bolted!'

'There probably isn't a catch on a window in this entire house that's secure. I climbed in through the scullery window,' he supplied grimly.

'You can go out by the front door. I'm feeling even less hospitable than I felt this afternoon,' she flared. 'You frightened me out of my wits!'

'Be glad it was me and not a real intruder. God, you can't be planning to stay here tonight!' Taking in the evidence around him, he glowered down at her. 'What are you doing here?'

'Why don't you go down the road and ask all your other neighbours what they're doing in their houses after midnight?' she returned angrily. 'You've got no right to walk in here.'

He bent his dark, arrogant head to avoid the shade on the central light above. 'I had no idea that you were here,' he growled. 'No idea at all.'

'Well, now that you've established that I'm not a gang of bikers in search of a new clubhouse, you are free to go.' Pointedly she sipped at her drink.

Long fingers coiled round the bottle. He gave it a cursory inspection, his mouth hardening. He straightened, sending her a savage look. 'You've picked up some bad habits since you left home.'

'You'll be relieved to know that one of them isn't inviting strange men to join me for a drink. Now will you get out of here?' Her voice rose steeply on the demand.

Jake lowered himself smoothly down into the chair at the foot of the mattress and crossed one booted ankle across his knee, stretching back in a relaxed pose that set her teeth on edge.

Incensed she got up on her knees. 'Did you hear what I said?'

The firelight glistened on the magenta silk shirt that came no lower than her shapely thighs, the thin fabric moulding the tip-tilted swell of her breasts. As she registered where those dark, intent eyes were resting without apology, her face burned. She sat back again, alarm bells ringing in her head.

'What are you doing here?' he asked again.

A sinuous, silk-clad shoulder shifted. 'Maybe I'm too lazy to shift to a hotel.'

'I'd have thought that comfort would have persuaded you to choose more suitable accommodation.' Cool, shrewd eyes studied her unreadably. 'What are you planning on doing now that you're out of *The Rothmans*?'

'If I'm out, I'm out by choice,' she snapped, flicked on the raw by his choice of words.

'As I understand it, Maxwell told you that if he had anything to do with it you wouldn't work ever again,' Jake reminded her with a calm that mocked her own loss of temper.

Her chin came up in a defensive thrust. 'I wanted some time off. I haven't had many holidays since you last saw me.'

'This is a peculiar location for a holiday.'

'Each to their own.' It was none of his business that she would be leaving again in the morning.

'Why the beat-up car?' he enquired idly.

She gave him a superior glance. 'It's camouflage. That's all.'

'As camouflage it's a little excessive.'

'Maybe I'm broke,' she parried with sarcastic bite. 'And this is the only place that I've got to go. Bring on the violins.'

The aggressive gleam in her eyes challenged him, letting him see just how much she resented his questions. His level gaze narrowed, faint colour aligning his hard cheekbones. As she had meant to, she had embarrassed him with her nonsensical response. For of course it was ridiculous. She had to resist a cringingly uncouth urge to tell him exactly what she was worth.

He rested his dark head back. 'It isn't healthy to drown your sorrows alone,' he drawled softly.

She arched a brow. 'I do unhealthy things all the time. They're usually the most fun.'

He loosed his breath audibly. 'Heaven sounds pretty painful at this time of night, Kitty. Does Maxwell know where you are?'

'He knew I was heading north.'

'I assume that you have split up with him.'

She let sherry moisten her throat. 'You're free to assume whatever you like. Grant and I have this unbreakable rule. We don't discuss each other with anybody. That's one of the reasons why there's so much rubbish in the papers. What can't be got through a legitimate interview is invented.'

'You don't say. Was the extraordinary revelation of the separate bedrooms made up?' Jake prompted silkily. 'Taking out the obvious exaggerations—I mean, I can't believe that you entertained his women, but I can believe that you bought his ties—well, in short it's obvious that the affair's been dead on his side for a very long time. So why were you still in residence?'

She stroked a forefinger over the open-weave blanket she was sitting on. 'So you read the papers. I suppose it was too much to hope that you wouldn't try to satisfy your curiosity at source.'

'Fascination would be a more apt tag for my feelings. Some of the bits relating to Maxwell were quite hilariously entertaining. But there were other parts next door to tragic,' he murmured bleakly. 'If he's finally chucked you out the door, he's done you a favour.'

'What would you know about it?' she exploded. 'You know nothing about my life with Grant. Nothing!'

He stared steadily back at her. 'You can't tell me that you've been happy with a man who's been running round with other women ever since you met him.'

Her delicate profile tensed. She gazed into the fire. All over again she was hearing Grant's raging and bitter accusations of ingratitude. She had turned down the surprise part he had offered her in his film, reiterating her ambition to become a writer. His fury had been perfectly understandable. He had taught her, encouraged her, pushed her hard when she would have dropped back. Everything she was today, she owed to him.

But Grant had still failed to give her the one thing that she really wanted from him. And that wasn't the adrenalin thrill of public recognition, the use of his luxurious homes or even the thousand and one costly gifts he continually pressed on her. It was a father's love she had wanted, not what that same father could give her in material terms.

Suddenly tears flooded her shadowed eyes. Perhaps it wasn't her father's fault, perhaps it was hers. There had to be some element lacking in her. The people she loved never loved her back. Grant had pulled the same rug from under her feet all over again.

'Kitty——'

'Oh, for God's sake, go away and leave me alone!' she gasped, despising her self-pitying mood. 'You've had your superior little say and now you can get out!'

With a sound of impatience he folded forward, settling down on the edge of the mattress to slant an arm round her hunched-up figure. 'I didn't intend to sound superior——'

'Didn't you?' she interrupted accusingly.

He sighed. 'God knows I don't receive any satisfaction from seeing you like this. I just don't think you should be on your own right now.'

The weight and warmth of his arm had shocked her into defensive rigidity, but as he plucked her glass away her overbright eyes flamed. 'What do you think you're doing?'

'I believe you've had enough.' Long fingers speedily enclosed her wrist, preventing her from retrieving the glass. 'Booze will only make you more depressed.'

At his peremptory bidding her hand had automatically withdrawn again. It infuriated her to appreciate that the habit of doing as Jake told her could have survived the years to exercise that influence. 'Two small glasses of sherry isn't boozing and I'm not depressed,' she rebutted stridently.

'No?' he queried.

'No! I've just had a rough couple of days.'

As he belatedly released her wrist he balanced his other hand on her shoulder. His touch remained, branding her sensitive skin. Bemusedly stilled by his disturbing nearness, she felt her breath tickle in her throat, her mind a sluggish mass of half-formed thoughts. As she glanced up, dimly wondering what was the matter with her, she connected with black-lashed golden eyes and a sliding sensation pulled at the pit of her stomach. Silence buzzed, broken only by the crackle of the fire. The pink tip of her tongue delved out to moisten the dryness of her lower lip.

Jake groaned, muttered something ferocious under his breath. His dark, hard features clenched, his glittering gaze burning over her upturned face. Something stronger and older and infinitely more powerful than she was held her utterly still as long fingers twined into her hair and his dark head bent.

His hand settled impatiently on her spine, tipping her back. His mouth parted hers with a hot, hard urgency that sent sensation coursing through her in wild, primitive response. His tongue thrust a demanding passage between her lips and her head spun. He was above her and then he lowered his long, hard-boned frame, his unmistakable maleness as he shuddered against her yielding curves, making her blood race and throb through her veins in delight. Suddenly her arms were closing round him in collusion and acceptance.

As he slid on to his side, he carried her with him. He continued to hungrily probe her mouth, his hand curving over her breast to invoke an electrifying excitement that dragged a sharp little cry unawares from her throat.

The old mantel clock high above wheezed and rang out a tinny stroke of one. Instantly both of them froze. Jake lifted away without warning, sinking back on his heels, his breathing thick and fast as he studied her with smouldering charcoal eyes.

Sitting up, Kitty gave herself a faint shake, smoothing down the rumpled shirt, abysmally conscious of the betraying peaks of her breasts and the shocking unsteadiness of her hands. Yet, even flushed and tumbled, she managed to look like an exotic little cat, grooming herself with controlled cool.

'The line you're looking for is, "God, what have I done?"' Never had Kitty's ready tongue come more welcomely to her rescue than in that intense, lacerating silence.

'Why the hell did you have to come back?' he demanded with a raw, unexpected violence that made her flinch, flat savagery in his eyes.

An antipathy as potent as the passion they had shared had sprung up with equal suddenness.

'I should keep this from Paula. Women are notoriously unforgiving creatures,' Kitty hissed back at him.

Colour seared his blunt cheekbones, accentuating eyes still brilliant with unsettled emotions. 'I was actually worried about you,' he derided with a curled lip.

'And just think, you don't even have a teeny glass of sherry to use as an excuse for your lapse.' She ignored the arrow of pain that that stinging taunt drove into her own heart.

He went white. 'You poisonous little bitch,' he bit out. 'If you think that I've ever forgotten that night, you're wrong. It's never left me.'

But it had not marked him as it had marked her. He had had a wife, a child and now he was back inside another relationship. Where were his scars? They didn't exist. Her head bent, silk-fine hair shimmering forward to hide her pinched profile. Dear heaven, why hadn't she felt physically ill when he had touched her?

'Go away,' she whispered.

'That is an invitation I don't need.' The door thudded on his exit.

She didn't hear a car start up. But then she hadn't heard one arriving. He must have walked up from the road, planning to take the intruder by surprise. Last of the macho heroes! Her bitter humour was short-lived. How could she respond to Jake when she couldn't respond to other men? Admittedly the latter situation had risen very rarely to be tested. Jake had burnt her so badly that she had shrunk from putting her hand in the fire again. Was that why she had stayed with Grant for so long? Had she been sheltering her own inadequacy? Was it really fair of her to have accused her father of using her?

When she had moved into the town house, it had never occurred to her that the world would assume she was Grant's mistress. She had honestly believed that, once she was presentable, Grant would be prepared to acknowledge their relationship openly. But Grant would never own up to fatherhood. He was extremely sensitive about his age, even more self-aware of his pin-up status. That he was closer to the half-century mark than forty was almost as big a secret as his possession of a twenty-five-year-old daughter.

And Kitty had become his defensive shield against persistent women. Kitty, though he had vehemently denied the accusation, was his excuse when one of his light-hearted affairs became too heavy. For so long all her energy had gone into her career. If she had been in no hurry to test herself out as an unattached woman, a large part of it had been lack of interest and the suspicion that she was frigid.

Frigid, she echoed dismally, shamed heat slinking through her in waves. Neither repulsion nor inhibition had attacked her in Jake's arms. Was she some kind of masochist? Where had that absolutely terrifying response come from? In all this time she had never forgotten the humiliation and shame that Jake's rejection had once taught her, forever afterwards making her repress her sexuality. She had feared an involvement with another man. She had to face that truth now.

Feeling intensely vulnerable, she curled up in a tight ball. Jake had hurt her savagely and those wounds were still raw. Drowsiness was overcoming her heavily. He was right, she allowed on her last coherent thought, I am depressed.

The aroma of coffee was in the air when she awakened. China rattled and she came bolt upright, clutching a quilt she didn't remember bringing downstairs. Her mattress had moved during the night as well. It was now several feet away from the fire. But what made those puzzling developments absolutely unimportant was the sight of Jake emerging from the scullery bearing two cups.

'What on earth . . . ?' she began incredulously.

'I was worried about you. I came back.' He set one of the cups down beside her on the floor and straightened lithely again to carry his own to his hard-set mouth.

Dark stubble shadowed his strong jawline. A half-unbuttoned shirt revealed a strip of tawny skin and a crisp sprinkling of black chest hair. Never had she been more achingly, agonisingly conscious of his disruptive sexuality. Some natural barrier had tumbled down since last night. Her pulses were racing in an atmosphere that suddenly felt unbearably claustrophobic.

'What time is it?' Disorientated, she had to say it twice to get it out and she studied the quilt, not even sure what day of the week it was.

'Half-eight.'

She pushed a hand through her hair. 'What's going on?'

'You were sleeping like the dead when I came back,' he asserted abrasively.

'Is there something wrong with sleeping in the middle of the night?' she muttered, seeking the cup with a blind hand. Her mouth was dry as a bone.

He released his breath in a sudden hiss. 'You should have woken up when I came back. You didn't. You obviously carried on drinking after I left.'

That did penetrate her mental fog. Her head flew up. 'I what?'

'You heard me. You were dead to the world.' Fierce anger laced each harsh syllable.

'Why don't you take your assumptions somewhere where they'll be less offensive?' she snapped, equally angry. 'I didn't have anything more to drink!'

A dubious dark brow elevated. 'No?'

She flung him an infuriated stare. 'No!' she repeated. 'Do you have any idea how long it is since I had a decent night's sleep? I was exhausted last night. I fell asleep within minutes of your departure.'

Dark eyes aimed a derisive and renewed challenge. 'You can still be grateful that I did come back. You left the candles burning. Didn't you realise that the electricity was only switched off at the meter? You didn't even put a guard up on that fire,' he informed her grimly. 'This house has wood partition walls. You're fortunate it wasn't your funeral pyre last night!'

Pale now, she hunched under the quilt, her hands cupped round the coffee. 'I'm not normally so careless, but if you're looking for gratitude, you're in the wrong place. Nobody asked you to interfere. How long have you been here?'

'Since about three,' he admitted shortly. 'I didn't like to leave you again until I was sure you were all right.'

Pinned to her mattress, sluggish and dishevelled, she felt grossly disadvantaged. 'Have you turned nocturnal?' she enquired. 'Won't someone have missed you?'

'Sophie's used to my being out at night.'

Really? He stayed overnight with Paula, did he? Times must have changed in Mirsby. You'd have been a scarlet woman the length and the breadth of the neighbourhood if you had behaved like that when Kitty had lived here. Hating him, she let coffee scald her tongue. Why wouldn't he leave her alone? Yesterday had been a truly ghastly day and Jake had clogged up far too much of it.

'Throw on some clothes. I'll take you home for breakfast. A neighbourly act,' he specified drily.

She nearly choked on her coffee. 'Breakfast?'

Abruptly he dropped down on a level with her. 'I've had enough drama in the last twenty-four hours to last me into the next century,' he warned abrasively. 'I also have a suggestion I want to put to you.'

'Keep it. Keep breakfast as well,' she advised, bending her head to evade a collision with rich, dark eyes far too close for comfort.

'Is it so hard for you even to be civil to me?' he raked, low and rough.

Her eyes closed. Every minute she spent in his radius heightened her inner turmoil. It would not be long before he questioned the depth of her bitter sensitivity to an episode he had firmly set behind him under the forgivable heading of misspent youth. She was terrified of exposing her vulnerability to that extent. But she would never be able to forgive him for the impossible choice he had once laid before her. How could she forget the agony of losing her baby?

Her eyelids smarted with sudden stinging moisture. That was a period of her life that she did not want to recall in his presence. It made her too vulnerable.

Jake expelled his breath, searching the drawn tension of her shielded profile. 'Look, I can understand that you feel pretty raw right now, but I'm not the enemy.'

With a shaken sound of disagreement, she pushed back the quilt. 'Give me ten minutes.'

CHAPTER THREE

Up in the bathroom Kitty shivered as she washed and tugged clothes on clumsily over goose-fleshed limbs. If she had one personal hate, it was a bathroom like a fridge. She combed her hair, grateful for the excellence of a cut that made the long, gleaming strands fall smoothly back into style. She rubbed her cheeks, saw some pink appear.

Downstairs again, she looked round the empty room thoughtfully. She could be comfortable enough here. She had hot and cold running water and the means to eat and keep warm. She wasn't so soft that she had to have the luxuries. As she tossed her toiletries bag back into her case, she noticed the phone sitting on one of the chairs tucked under the table and she smiled. Now that was a necessity.

She climbed into the Range Rover, slim and bright in her black jeans and a red sweater, worn under a soft leather jerkin. His cloaked gaze whipped over her, leaving her feeling curiously self-conscious.

'When did Gran get the phone in?' she asked.

'I persuaded her to get it in after your grandfather died,' Jake answered, filtering the vehicle slowly down the lane to avoid the deepest pot-holes. 'I'm fairly certain she never used it, but it gave her a feeling of security.'

Kitty had stiffened. 'Something else I need to thank you for?'

'I don't want your thanks,' he parried flatly. 'To get down to my suggestion—I think you ought to stay up at Torbeck for a few days.'

In sharp disconcertion she turned to look at him. 'At your farm?'

His hard-set profile was impassive. 'As I understood it, you've nowhere else to go until you get yourself sorted out.'

She stole a startled glance at him under her lashes, oxygen trapped in her convulsed throat. Dear heaven, had he taken her derisive plea of poverty seriously last night? Only a spendthrift fool could have been broke after the well-paid employment she had enjoyed. Too late she recalled how the Press had lovingly interpreted Grant's roared assurance that without him she wouldn't have a penny to bless herself with. Furthermore, Jake had two sisters and a mother, who had reputedly run up debts everywhere locally before he had been able to convince them that they could no longer afford the costly extras they had once taken for granted. Jake had no experience of women possessed of financial common sense.

Carefully she breathed in, oddly reluctant to subject him to the full absurdity of his misapprehension. 'You know, I was joking last night. I'm not suffering from a cash-flow problem, Jake.'

He interrupted her drily, paying no heed to her firmly voiced assurance. 'Possibly the invitation didn't come out quite as I intended, but it was well meant. You need peace and privacy right now. It's available at Torbeck. Sophie spends half her day in bed and the other half down at Merrill's. You're welcome to take up the offer. There are no strings attached to it, if that's what you're worried about.'

'No, that wasn't what——'

'I won't touch you again. Neither of us really knew what we were doing last night,' he cut in grimly.

'Speak for yourself.' Did he have a whole list of excuses? she wondered in disgust. I was drunk; I didn't know what I was doing. Did maniacal passion resulting in temporary insanity only strike him in her radius?

Something far from cold had leapt into his incisive gaze. 'You mean it didn't matter who it was? Any port in a storm?'

Tempted to slap the unpleasant smile off his darkly handsome features, she curled her fingers tightly into her palm. 'I wouldn't know. I'm not a sailor.'

'You're right there,' he conceded smoothly. 'You were drowning last night.'

The muscles in her stomach contracted sickly. Had he noticed something surprisingly inexperienced in her response? Determined not to show her shrinking discomfiture over the suspicion, she breathed mockingly, 'Did that give you a buzz? I like men. Do you have a problem with that, Jake? Human sexual response is all about pressing the right buttons, and you're not exactly without virtuosity in the field, are you?' Warming up, she let a languorous smile form on her lips. 'Surely you're not complaining because I enjoyed the demonstration?'

A white tension had hardened his jawline. 'You sound like a tramp.'

'No, you don't like women who enjoy it. Do I make you feel threatened in some way?' Kitty dealt him a condescendingly interested appraisal from beneath her curling lashes. 'Do you need the pretence of fumbling innocence to turn you on? Is that what Paula——'

The Range Rover suddenly shot to a bone-jolting emergency stop. Snaking out both his hands, he yanked her forward. Wide-eyed and pale, she stared up at him. Rage burned in his blazing dark scrutiny. His hand rested with whiplash accuracy against her slender throat. 'Leave Paula out of this. One more word and, so help me God, Kitty, I'll...'

'You'll what?' Shaken by the tenor of her own cheap taunts, she was trembling. But on a secret level a hand-in-the fire exhilaration had gripped her to power her through her verbal assault on his masculinity.

Abruptly his hands left her. 'That is one bait I won't bite. No games, Kitty. I warn you,' he gritted.

Sliding back, she jerked a shoulder, mutinously silent. At least her scornful attack had obliterated any unfortunate impression she might have left behind. Woodenly she stared out of the windscreen. Games? That was his department. Or it had been eight years ago. Stop it...stop it, a voice shrieked inside her head. Eight years ago, Kitty. Eight years ago.

Brown fingers drummed a soundless tattoo on the wheel. Without looking at him, she could tell that he was shaken up as well. The vibrations in the air were suffocating. 'We don't have to be at each other's throats. I want to be a friend. That is all,' he said roughly.

'Don't put your hand on a Bible and say it if you're hoping to get through the Pearly Gates unchallenged.'

He bit out a humourless laugh. 'You've got no make-up on and you ought to look like hell after the last week, but you're still the most beautiful woman I've ever known. Is that what your ego needs to hear from me?' he demanded scathingly. 'Is that what you wanted last night? You don't need that confirmation from me or anybody else.'

Unmovingly she watched him, her oval face clean of all expression. Her looks had brought her more disillusionment than happiness. Beauty had been a necessary passport into her father's superficial affections. It had been her possibilities, not her personality which had persuaded Grant to take her under his wing.

And if she hadn't been beautiful, Jake would have left her alone. At seventeen she had been defenceless. He had not even needed to lie about loving her to have his careless hour of satisfaction. There was nothing she would have denied him then. The knowledge made her stomach clench.

'Will you stay at Torbeck?' he prompted impatiently.

For a malicious second she savoured the prospect of his mother's horror should she be saddled with her as a houseguest. Paula wouldn't like it too much either. As quickly as she pictured the havoc she could wreak, she discarded the unattractive vision.

'I'm going to stay at Lower Ridge,' she told him flatly.

In the act of moving on the Range Rover, he stopped, his dark head whipping back to her in shock. 'You can't be serious!' he said forcefully. 'The house is falling down. The wiring's dangerous.'

'The house has stood for many years. I doubt if it will burn, blow up or collapse round my ears in the space of a few months,' she scoffed.

'A few months?' he ejaculated. 'Why the hell would you stay that long?'

'I have plans which don't entail returning to my career as an actress.' Angrily she surveyed him, pushing up her chin in unconscious challenge. 'I'm planning to write a book.'

A derisive incredulity slashed his taut features. 'On the men you have known? You'd be wiser keeping your mouth shut.'

He didn't remember the stories she used to scribble in her teens. He didn't remember a dream she had been too shy to share with anyone but him. 'Don't worry, Jake. You won't even get a footnote.'

Simmering with pain and indignation, she dug her shaky hands into her pockets.

In the charged silence he grated, 'I'll buy the farm from you. The money can be raised fast. You don't need to hang around up here.'

'No, thanks. You don't like the idea of me as a neighbour much, do you?'

His teeth glimmered white against bronzed skin and it absently occurred to her that not even prolonged outdoor exposure to the elements had given him that depth of a tan in a Yorkshire winter. 'How do you expect me to feel about it?'

Her violet-blue eyes stayed steady. 'I don't expect you to feel anything.'

Once she had paid the price of exile for him. Never again. He wanted the farm. It wouldn't suit him if she began getting ideas of keeping it on as a holiday cottage. Of course he didn't know that she could afford to entertain ideas of that nature. He didn't know that if she wanted the land to be put to profitable use, she could place it in the hands of a highly professional outfit not so very far from where they were sitting. How would he react to the news that she owned the Grange and most of the original Tarrant estate?

Grant had bought it for her as a surprise. Her father was a multimillionaire, who had enjoyed a large financial stake in the profits of his own films. What had struck her as a shatteringly costly purchase had been no more than a flamboyant gesture on his part. He had termed it a superb investment for her future security. But that wasn't why he had bought the estate for her. Grant had honestly believed that she would receive a venomous kick from owning Jake's former family home.

They were now travelling up a concrete lane. A long black and white farmhouse sat on a pleasant rise among a grove of stark winter branched trees. In spring, Torbeck was probably very attractive, she allowed grudgingly.

'I'm sorry if I was rough on you back there, but you're a complication I can do without,' he admitted shortly.

Climbing out of the car, she said, 'I'm not your complication.'

'You stir up things I'd prefer to forget.' His well-shaped mouth twisted. 'I don't think you'll stick Lower

Ridge longer than a week in this weather. I'll stay clear while you're there though.'

As he pressed open the porch door, she chided, 'Promises, promises.'

A child was sitting on the bottom step of the stairs in the spacious hall. An instantaneous freezing coldness encased Kitty from neck to toe. Amazingly, she had forgotten about the existence of Jake's daughter. Mousy hair, freckles and thick-lensed spectacles contrived to make her a surprisingly plain little girl. The Tarrants were without exception a physically very handsome bunch. This one wasn't.

'Why aren't you at playgroup?' Jake demanded in surprise. 'Tina?'

''Cos I's waiting for my lift and it didn't come.'

Jake frowned darkly. 'I'll take you. Sorry, Kitty, this is Tina.'

'Hello, Tina.' Kitty just about managed to glance in the child's direction.

'You're pretty,' Tina mumbled and nervously eyed her father. 'I don't wanna go to playgroup.'

'You're going.'

Without warning Tina burst into floods of tears. A phone started shrilling somewhere. With a muffled curse, Jake swept Tina off her perch in a mixture of frustration and sympathy. 'Please, Daddy, please,' she sobbed.

'Tina ... for crying out loud.'

The phone had stopped ringing. A large, plump woman clad in a floral pinny came into the hall. 'You didn't grow up aways, did you?' Jessie noted bluntly as she studied Kitty, quite indifferent to the racket Tina was making. 'And you're skin and bone.'

Kitty laughed, her coolness vanishing. Jake's features hardened as he watched the vibrancy flash back into her lovely face.

'You won't be getting your breakfast yet,' the older woman angled at her employer. 'That was John on the phone. Starlight's foaling. He wants someone to hold his hand.'

'It looks as if you'll be eating in peace after all,' Jake breathed. 'I'd better get changed. By the way, what happened to Tina's lift?'

'Mrs Crummer's kids are down with that flu that's doing the rounds,' Jessie delivered with the gruesome air of the hangman. 'You'd best hope it stops there.'

Jake started upstairs carting Tina. Her mournful little face stabbed guilt knives into Kitty over his shoulder. Swiftly she looked away.

'And don't go out without ringing Paula!' Jessie rolled her eyes heavenward. 'That phone hasn't stopped ringing this morning.'

Kitty followed her into a sunny pine kitchen. 'You weren't surprised to see me.'

'His nibs phoned. Get yourself sat down. We don't stand on ceremony here.'

Shedding her jacket, Kitty slid uncertainly behind the table in the alcove. 'Perhaps Jake ought to drop me back again now.'

Jessie slapped a mug of tea down in front of her. 'The meal's ready for you. He shouldn't be long. John Thornton's a fusspot. He probably doesn't need him at all.'

'Thornton? The auctioneer?' A plate piled high with bacon, sausage and egg was withdrawn from the oven and placed before her. 'Jessie, I couldn't possibly eat all this!'

Ignoring her startled plea, Jessie replied, 'Young John, not old John. He went into farming. Jake and him are partners. He's Merrill's husband. She's expecting her first this summer.'

Kitty lifted her knife and fork. 'What happened to Jane?' she asked, referring to Jake's older sister.

'She married an American, did well for herself. He's one of those fancy private doctors—plenty of brass,' Jessie emphasised in case she hadn't got the message.

Kitty smiled. The housekeeper busied herself down at the dishwasher, giving her peace to eat.

Tina sidled out from behind the cupboards to stare at Kitty wide-eyed. 'I know you. You're the witch on TV,' she whispered, half fearful, half fascinated.

Charming, Kitty thought, idly wondering who in the household might have alluded to her in the child's hearing with a similar-sounding word.

'None of your silly nonsense.' Jessie bent a stern look on the little mite just as Jake reappeared.

'I won't be long. Tina!' A hand jerked meaningfully. He barely broke his stride on his passage to the back door.

In ten seconds both father and daughter were gone. His terse manner had annoyed Kitty. 'What's up with him?'

'Woman trouble.'

Kitty buttered a piece of toast, her appetite improving. 'What's this Paula like?'

'Divorced. She took one look at him and set her cap,' Jessie informed her while she noisily stacked dishes. 'Not that I've anything against the lass, but chasing him up hill and down dale isn't the path to take to the church door.'

'Serious, then, is it?' Kitty pried helplessly.

'I reckon she is. I can't speak for him. He doesn't wear his thoughts on his sleeve. The wee one could certainly do with a mother. Miss Sophie's got no time for her at all. It would suit all round if he did get wed again,' Jessie pronounced with practicality. 'Miss Sophie could go and live with that sister of hers in York. She's forever visiting her. It's too quiet up here for her.'

'Then why does she stay?'

Jessie sighed. 'I don't live in now. My brother's pushing seventy-five. Since his wife died, I've been keeping house for him. Jake has to have somebody in the house at night for the child in case he's called out.'

Kitty glanced up. 'Called out where?'

'He's one of the local vets. Didn't you know that?'

Kitty shook her head. 'Last I heard, he had to leave university.'

'You've not been doing a lot of talking, have you?' Jessie remarked drily. 'He was near the end of his training. Once he had this place going, he went back and finished it. He can only manage part time though. What with building up the farm ... well, he stretched himself in all directions. He had to in the beginning. His father owed all round him when he died.'

'He hasn't had an easy time of it,' Kitty muttered.

Jessie gave a vigorous nod of agreement. 'He hasn't. Miss Sophie took losing her husband very hard. She had one of those breakdowns and she's not been the same since. She never took to Liz either. That didn't help.'

Kitty bit her lip and bent her head to eat. A good five minutes passed before her companion spoke again.

'Like a lot of folk round here, I've often wondered what went wrong between you and Jake,' Jessie confided brusquely.

Kitty tensed. 'I can't think why. I was just a kid when I left. Jake and I never even went out together.'

Jessie gave her a strange look, turned aside. 'Happen not.'

Crimson rose in Kitty's cheeks.

'I never saw two young people that keen and nothing come of it.' Jessie was not to be silenced. 'If it was some silly argument that parted you, you needed your heads

banged together and you oughtn't to pay heed to that
rumour that he married young Liz for her money. Not
that I could tell you why he did marry her, but you take
it from me, it certainly wasn't for that.'

Kitty's teeth had collided painfully with her tongue.
Her mouth tasted of blood.

'Yes,' Jessie grumbled. 'He married in haste and re-
pented at his leisure, as they say. Liz was that jealous
of you.'

'I never even met the woman!' Kitty burst out.

'That's no call to go raising your voice against me,'
Jessie sniffed. 'I don't care if you are on the television
every week. You mind your manners.'

Laughter and tears simultaneously clogged her throat.
'I'm sorry, Jessie.'

Jake had married for money. How simple, how
understandable, how neat. Why had she not suspected
that hard cash might lie behind his sudden marriage?
Nausea cramped her stomach and she pushed away her
plate. Of course, he could have loved her as well. Easier
to love where it's profitable, a more cynical voice piped
up. With the estate teetering on bankruptcy and his
family to provide for, some might say that Jake had had
plenty of excuse.

A bell sounded, making Kitty jump. Jessie bustled out
into the utility corridor visible beyond the glassed rear
door. Distantly Kitty heard the drone of a male voice.
Jessie returned with a slim, fair-haired man in tow.

'Drew Matcham,' she proffered baldly. 'He works with
Jake.'

'I twisted Jessie's arm for an introduction when I saw
you through the kitchen window,' he confessed rather
awkwardly.

'She's not even had her breakfast yet,' Jessie scolded
without pity.

'It's all right, I was finished.' Kitty got up and clasped his less than confidently extended hand.

He stared at her in astonishment. 'Good lord, you're really tiny. I assumed the rest of the cast was very tall.'

As he reddened comically over his own candour, she couldn't help smiling. 'The high heels helped on set,' she laughed. 'I didn't think many men watched the show.'

His hazel eyes twinkled. 'I've got to admit that I don't, but I've caught the odd glimpse when my sister's been watching. Well...' He hesitated, openly angling for the offer of a cup of tea, but Jessie was loudly slotting cutlery in a drawer. 'Well, since Jake's out, I'll get on,' he completed.

'Will you be travelling near the Tarn road?' Kitty asked impulsively and, at his surprised nod of affirmation, continued, 'Would you mind giving me a lift?'

'Not at all.'

Tugging on her jacket, she evaded Jessie's shocked stare. Coming here had been a mistake. If she lingered, Jessie would soon be happily filling her in on every aspect of Jake's marriage. Kitty really didn't want to hear any more gory details.

She told the housekeeper that she had hugely enjoyed her breakfast, smoothly pointed out that she wanted to save Jake the inconvenience of driving her home, and concluded her speech by asking Jessie to assure Mrs Tarrant that she was very sorry to have missed her. In short she told three huge whoppers in unblushing succession.

'I picked up the wrong end of the stick,' Drew murmured as she slid into his car. 'I assumed you were a guest here.'

Kitty waved brightly at Jessie. 'I'm staying at Lower Ridge farm.'

'I've heard of it but I've never been up there.'

'What did you hear?' she enquired.

'That it was the birthplace of homegrown talent,' he fielded lightly.

She relaxed perceptibly as Torbeck receded behind them. Drew chatted about the rumour that snow was in the air and she liked him for not asking nosy questions. Passing down these same roads an hour earlier, she had been too enervated to notice the changes in the landscape. Now that she did, her brow furrowed. 'What happened to the trees that used to be along here?'

'Bob Creighton happened,' Drew supplied. 'He manages the old Tarrant estate. He took down those trees in spite of local opposition.'

Kitty swallowed uneasily. 'He can't be too popular, then.'

'I wouldn't say that,' Drew said mildly. 'The estate provides a lot of local employment and it's run on a maximum productivity basis. Bob has to turn in decent profits if he wants to hang on to his job. He says his bosses function entirely on balance sheets. He doesn't see much of them. They're based in London.'

'He must have a pretty free hand,' she commented stiffly.

Drew glanced at her. 'Has Jake been talking to you? He was furious about those trees, although he refused to head up the opposition party.'

'He can't have been too bothered, then.'

Drew sighed in rueful disagreement. 'He was in a very difficult position after the estate was sold. A lot of people still find it hard to accept that Jake's got nothing to do with it now. They tend to try to involve him in their problems.'

Kitty lifted her chin. 'There were plenty of problems while his father was alive.'

'But the situation is similar. An absentee landlord or landlords,' Drew filled in thoughtfully. 'And you can't underestimate what the name of Tarrant still stands for in this neck of the woods.'

'Oh, I don't. I'm sure there are still a lot of farmers pulling their cloth caps off when Jake walks into the yard.'

Unexpectedly Drew laughed, taking her vitriolic stab as a joke. 'Yes, I've had to get used to being second best with some of our clients.'

'Who lives in the Grange now?' she prompted.

'It's empty. There hasn't been a tenant there for a while.'

She insisted that he drop her at the foot of the lane. 'I feel like the walk,' she said truthfully.

She thought uncomfortably over what she had learnt of how the estate was viewed locally. Her investment consultants had set up Colwell Holdings, the management firm which ran the estate for her. She received regular reports which she rarely even bothered to read, and all of a sudden she wished that she hadn't gone to such lengths to conceal her ownership. Even Creighton didn't know who was behind Colwell Holdings. She deeply resented being compared to Charles Tarrant, but she couldn't deny that she had had no real interest in the estate.

Haggerston Grange was empty, she reflected. She might as well go up and take a look round the old house. Why shouldn't she? It belonged to her.

She entered the cottage, experiencing only a pang of yesterday's reluctance. She was staying, come rain, hail or shine. If anything, Jake's objections had only hardened her resolve. Any ghosts here were of her own creation. Why had she let Jake and then Jessie upset her?

In essentials Jake seemed unchanged. His past behaviour had to have an uneasy hold on his conscience. Why else had he forced himself to offer the hand of charity? A friend, he had said. Where had this friendship been when she had so desperately needed him? Having slept with her, Jake had made it cruelly clear that even friendship was at an end. Her eyes dampened and in annoyance she wrinkled her nose.

Sophie Tarrant had ironically picked out what Kitty now saw as her greatest weakness. She was too intense. Any normal woman would have put the past behind her by now. She would never have returned here. Why was she here? Why was that past still hurting her? She couldn't answer those questions.

Another scrunched up ball of paper hit the floor. With a grimace Kitty left her typewriter. It had ruled her every waking hour for a week. That first chapter which had seemed so clear in her head refused to emerge on to the printed page and satisfy her. She had seen nothing but these four walls for days. Pulling on her raincoat, she decided to go for a walk.

Maybe Grant had been right, maybe that one story had been a fluke. She trudged out into the drizzling rain, deep in her own thoughts. A noise eerily reminiscent of a child crying made her hesitate by the wall bounding the old vegetable patch and stare across the yard. The hair prickled at the nape of her neck. There was no wind. The barn was securely padlocked. Beside it sat a tumbledown outhouse that had once been a tractor shed. Just as she was about to turn away, smiling at her own fancies, the sound came again.

The door of the shed was hanging drunkenly off its hinges. Kitty peered into the dimness. In the corner, on a heap of old meal bags, she could just make out a small, recumbent shape. As she heaved the door back, it gave a wrenching shriek of complaint. Tina leapt up fearfully to cringe back into the corner.

Kitty stated at her in astonishment. The child was wringing wet and caked with mud. She didn't even have a cardigan on over her torn blouse and kilt. Her swollen face crumpled into another heartbroken sob.

Her distress unfroze Kitty. 'It's all right, I'm not cross.' She dropped down on her knees in an effort to seem less intimidating. 'You're a long way from home and I was just surprised to see you. How did you get here?'

'W... walked,' Tina gasped out hoarsely on the peak of another frightened sob.

Ran, Kitty translated, eyeing the ripped sleeve on the blouse and the angry scratch on the skin beneath. She must have fallen as well to have ended up in such a sorry state.

'You gave me a fright,' Kitty confided.

'Me?' Tina struggled against another sob.

Kitty nodded. 'Wasn't that silly of me?'

'No. I'm scared of lots and lots of things!' Tina wailed shakily.

Kitty abandoned her attempt at a psychological approach and put her arms round the shivering child. 'You mustn't be scared of me,' she muttered awkwardly.

Tina went rigid, but under the influence of soothing murmurs she chose to cling instead and cry all the harder. She was far too worked up to calm down quickly. Kitty took her in by the fire and lost no time in stripping her sodden clothing off. She tugged a rug off the settee which she had moved through from the parlour and wrapped Tina into its warm folds, frowning as she noticed the slap marks imprinted on one skinny little leg. Anger stirred in Kitty. Surely a rebuke would have been sufficient to discipline a child as timid as Tina?

She lifted the phone book. 'I'm going to phone your house. Your granny must be worried about you.'

'Don't wanna go home,' Tina mumbled.

'Don't you want to see Daddy?' Kitty cajoled.

'Daddy's only home when I'm asleep,' Tina gulped wretchedly. 'I don't wanna go home. I'll get smacked again.'

The phone was answered by Jessie, her voice betrayingly sharp with strain. 'It's Kitty. Have you been looking for Tina? She's here at Lower Ridge with me.'

'Oh, thank God,' the older woman gasped. 'Is she all right? I've been looking everywhere for her.'

'She's fine. Wet and in a bit of a state, but no harm done.'

'It's been one of those days. I was packing for Miss Sophie's visit to her sister's and, while I was busy, Tina broke an ornament in the drawing-room. Miss Sophie lost her temper. When she'd left, I went up to bring Tina down from her room but she was gone,' Jessie relived the experience.

'How long has she been missing?'

'Could you bring her home?' In her flustered state, Jessie talked over her. 'I couldn't reach Jake. He's out on a call.'

Obeying her own instincts, Kitty first persuaded Tina into a warm bath. Between hiccups, she heard all about the ornament and how nobody liked bad little girls. She rolled up the sleeves of one of her sweaters to adapt it for Tina's use. By the time a plaster was fixed to her arm and she had had a cup of cocoa, Tina was losing her shyness. However, the moment she realised she was going home again, the tears returned and Kitty had to bundle her into the car.

The Range Rover was parked at Torbeck. Assuming that Jake was out in the other vehicle, Kitty lifted Tina unhurriedly from her car. Before she could reach the door, Jake came striding out, black temper etched into the rigidity of his strong features. When he saw Kitty standing there with Tina in her arms, he stilled. 'I was just on my way over to pick her up.'

Jessie emerged from the house at a trot. Bypassing Jake, she hurried forward and immediately reached for Tina. 'A fine dance you've led me this morning, young lady,' she scolded.

Tina loosed a gulping sob and clutched frantically at Kitty, whose sympathy had been of the more obvious variety. Jessie bore off the distraught child to the accompaniment of tearing sobs which Kitty found extremely upsetting.

'I'm sorry that you've been inconvenienced like this.' The apology clearly cost Jake an effort. It was patently obvious that he would rather his daughter had run in any direction other than Lower Ridge. 'Sometimes I don't know what gets into Tina.'

Kitty raised a brow. 'You don't?'

His jawline squared. 'She's very highly strung. Jessie's inclined to be a little too strict.'

'It wasn't Jessie who frightened the child into running away.' Uneasily, Kitty turned back to the car, prepared to go no further.

'Meaning?'

'Forget it,' she muttered.

A hand clamped to her shoulder, spinning her back with an easy strength that infuriated her. 'Are you saying that I was to blame?' It was raw. 'I wasn't even at home.'

'From what I've heard, you're not here very often,' Kitty returned dulcetly. 'But it's none of my business.'

'You're damned right, it's not!' Tawny anger emblazoned his fierce, narrowed scrutiny. 'For somebody who couldn't even bring herself to look at Tina last week, you're very concerned all of a sudden.'

Guilt attacked her. At first glimpse of Tina, an agonised bitterness had rushed up out of Kitty's subconscious. Today she had reacted instinctively to an unhappy child in need of comfort. Fond as she was of children, she was ashamed of that initial alienated response and deeply disturbed that Jake should have noticed her revealing lack of warmth.

'I've never had very much to do with young children,' she parried weakly.

'Yet you still think that you have the experience to judge me an inadequate father?' he bit out savagely.

No cooler now in temper, Kitty sent him a contemptuous smile. 'Well, to be brutally frank, I'm not over-impressed by what I've seen so far, and I was even less impressed when you left your housekeeper to deal with her just now.' She paused, undaunted by the expression of sheer incredulity on his dark visage. 'No, you don't like it when the boot's on the other foot, do you, Jake? You don't like being condemned without a fair hearing. Now you can understand how you've made me feel in the past.'

'A woman who conducts a particularly public affair with a man of Maxwell's age and reputation can't possibly be that sensitive.' His stare was insolently steady on her whitening face.

Her palm connected with his cheekbone. The blow was instinctive and the sting of the slap carried right up her arm. He didn't even flinch.

'So we are that sensitive,' he gibed, danger sparks entering an atmosphere already overcharged with hostility.

CHAPTER FOUR

KITTY was trembling, badly shaken by her complete loss of control. 'Much as I might like to stand here trading insults, I've got better things to do with my time,' she said tightly.

Hard fingers lifted at speed to snap round her narrow wrists, preventing her from walking away. 'And I've got a better idea for entertainment,' Jake blazed down at her.

Employing an ease that outraged her pride, he repelled her puny attempts to free herself and pulled her against his long, powerful length. The heat of his body penetrated her clothing. Her every nerve-ending leapt into an instant overload of shattering physical awareness. Her lips framed tart words of rejection and a crazy heat sprang up in her loins, her heartbeat suddenly thunder in her ears. She didn't know what she said. The hand clamped to the base of her spine impelled her into stirring contact with the hard thrust of his thighs and her knees went weak.

A kind of feverish panic claimed her. Involuntarily she collided with dark mahogany eyes. 'No...' The syllable was slurred.

He raised her up to him and covered her mouth with devastating urgency. Excitement possessed her. A jolt of such wild, tearing hunger followed in its wake that there was no room for all those frantic angry thoughts in her head... those thoughts that should have been there but somehow weren't. She was in his arms and she didn't know how she had got there. She couldn't think, she could only feel. Her fingers sank into his black hair, rejoicing in the thick, silky texture. Her head tipped back, unerringly providing him with easier access, and the passionate fusion of his mouth on hers was ecstasy.

On some distant level of unconcern she was aware that he swept her up and carried her out of the rain which was dampening her skin. When he settled her down again, something oddly coarse and springy met her spine, but the hand skimming impatiently beneath her sweater was more than capable of driving out that faint discomfort. He thrust the barrier of her clothing away and the burning heat of his mouth engulfed the aching peak of her nipple. A startled cry broke from her. A slow, spreading heat flickered and flamed deep down inside her.

He moaned her name and tasted her swollen lips once more with the same incredible hunger that was controlling her. It was a hunger that had no beginning and no end and, somewhere in the midst of it, they were both irretrievably lost. He ground his hips into her softer curves in a movement that made him shudder violently. He groaned something inaudible and then he swore, freeing her fast of his drugging weight.

Cool air washed her exposed skin. Jessie's call crossed the yard, loud and clear as a tannoy. Awareness returned to Kitty with the impact of a punch on the stomach. She clawed her sweater down clumsily, straightened her rucked skirt.

'You make me feel like an animal.' His savage confession sliced through the simmering silence. 'But that's what you've wanted from the start, isn't it?'

A horse shied nervously in a nearby stall. They were in a stable. She wanted to cringe in self-disgust but pride wouldn't let her. Nothing other than force would have made her look in his direction. She rose with what little dignity she could muster from a bed of flattened straw.

A ruthless hand snapped round her forearm, jerking her back against the brick wall. She almost fell. Her legs were as wobbly as an accident victim's and, just like an accident victim, she couldn't yet believe what had happened to her.

'Isn't it?' Hard fingers pushed up her chin, enforcing the visual contact she had shrunk from. A powerful anger simmered in the darkness of his fierce gaze and she felt dizzy again.

'I don't know what you're getting at.'

'Like hell you don't!' he derided. 'From the first moment outside the cemetery, you've been supremely, smugly self-aware that you can make me want you again. I can still see you draping yourself over that pillar like a Venus's fly-trap... just daring me to touch you.'

'A... A what?' She was defenceless under the attack. She couldn't think straight. In the space of a few crazed minutes, her entire conception of herself had exploded into nothingness, leaving her reeling inside a stranger's body.

He vented a harsh laugh. 'It wasn't intended as a compliment. I was actually stupid enough that day to think it was all an act. The walk, the megawatt smile, the "come close and get burnt" look in your eyes. I've seen you do it on TV and you do it well——' he spelt out with rich, unhidden contempt '—the come-on and then the put-down.'

When she made a desperate attempt to slide past him, a strong hand settled on her narrow shoulder to hold her demeaningly captive.

'Let me go!' she spat in panic.

'You weren't in the notion of going anywhere five minutes ago, so don't tell me you're pushed for time now!'

Heat suffused her pallor in a telling wave.

'My God, Kitty can still blush. Of course, there's something rather inglorious about the stable setting.' Smoothly master of himself once more, Jake was coldly cruel as she had never known him before. 'Tell me, when were you planning to call time? I wasn't playing one of your little power games, Kitty. I would have had you and to hell with the consequences!'

She gulped strickenly. 'You conceited b——'

His other hand braced against the wall as she shifted restively. 'Do you think so? Someone told me recently that it was just a matter of pushing the right buttons and it must be true. What's wrong, Kitty?' he chided silky soft, returning her provocation with interest. 'Do I make you feel threatened in some way?'

She shut her eyes tightly, willing him to leave her alone. Depsite his outer cool, she sensed the subdued violence still pent up just below the surface. The passion that had run riot between them had disturbed him just as deeply. But Jake had changed. How facile of her to imagine otherwise! She didn't recognise this abrasively masculine and menacing stranger, cutting her to ribbons with his tongue.

'You used to do that when you were a little girl.' His dark-timbred voice fractured into roughness. 'And now you're all grown up and supposedly able to look after yourself, I still want you so badly that I ache. Does that make you feel better? Does that satisfy you, Kitty? But I'm not taking the heat for Maxwell and I'm not planning to play substitute either,' he delivered forcefully. 'So what do you want from me?'

Even with her deliberately heavy steps neither of them had heard Jessie's approach. She coughed loudly and both of them spun, Jake springing back from Kitty to finally give her breathing space.

'I put Tina down for a nap and she's pleading for Kitty to come and tuck her in. She's taken quite a fancy to you.' Kitty received a veiled look that lingered. 'You'd best get that straw out of your hair.'

'Thank you, Jessie.' Jake's inflexion was Arctic.

'If you want to make a spectacle of yourself in the yard, you draw the kitchen curtains,' Jessie advised bluntly. 'I'm not blind.'

Her cheeks a wild-rose pink, Kitty plucked hurriedly at the offending piece of straw snarled up in her hair.

'I'll take you upstairs.' Jake thrust the back door wide.

Overtly conscious of him, Kitty felt a shiver travel through her tensed limbs. A flashfire recall of the hunger that had demanded and consumed her to the exclusion of all else nearly froze her in her tracks. No, don't think now, you can't afford to think now...here...

'I'll see to that,' Jessie overruled, bustling forward.

Tina was a minor lump in an overlarge three-quarter bed. Myopic eyes squinted at Kitty over the top of the sheet. A watery smile formed. 'Can I have a story?'

A tattered version of *The Ugly Duckling* appeared from under the covers. 'Daddy says when I grow up I'll be a beautiful swan,' Tina shared shyly. 'You can sit here.' The bed was patted and when Kitty had begun to read Tina whispered, 'You can put your arm round me if you like. Daddy does that. It's nice.'

Kitty rearranged herself. Tina snuggled up against her. 'I like you.' She hesitated. 'Do you like me?'

'Of course I like you.' The story, Kitty acknowledged, came a poor second to Tina's need for affection and reassurance.

The child giggled sleepily over the exaggerated animal noises Kitty used to liven up the text. Long before the end of the story, Tina was fast asleep. As Kitty stood up, she was dismayed to see Jake's tall, dark silhouette shadowing the doorway. How long had he been there watching her act the clown for his daughter's amusement?. she wondered in angry embarrassment.

'You do a masterly imitation of a cross mother duck,' he said as she shut the door behind her.

She spun defensively. 'I happen to like children.'

A sardonic twist moulded his firm lips. 'Isn't it strange that I should have received the impression that you would dislike any child of mine?'

Her breath caught in her throat. 'That's a crazy idea,' she parried, striving to inject the correct note of disdain into her intonation.

Unmoved by her scornful retort, he stared measuringly down at her. 'You're like tempered steel under the overwhelmingly feminine exterior. If you're not trying to put me down, you're on the attack. I find myself wondering why that should be after all this time...'

Her violet eyes were shuttered pools of vibrant colour in her stilled face. Suddenly she couldn't breathe and she was sick with fear. Jake turned the tables with a vengeance. Cool, clear intelligence powered his dark, perceptive scrutiny and froze up the muscles in her throat.

'Why?' The low-pitched demand rattled down her spine like castanets at a funeral. 'If I shook you again out from behind that glossy, oh, so superficial façade, would the girl I remember make a guest appearance? I refuse to believe that you've changed out of all recognition.'

He was close again—too close. A treacherous, conscienceless tide of yearning was rising inside her. It was the way he was looking at her, the dangerous undertow of tension threatening to suck her down. Under that dark glittering onslaught, her breasts swelled into uncomfortable tightness beneath her sweater. That awesome sexual current was uncontrollable and petrifying. She forced her feet on to the head of the stairs. It was the most difficult movement she had ever made in her life.

A piece of invisible elastic wanted to yank her relentlessly back to him.

'Kitty.'

Her name, and nobody else had ever said it with that exact inflexion. He was nowhere near her now and still she felt cornered. Once, unforgettably, the Tarrant coolheadedness had triumphed over his desire for the Colgan brat. The lesson ought to be engraved in letters of fire on her forehead. It ought to have killed stone-dead the shameful excitement he unleashed in her. That it did not was devastating Kitty all over again.

Fighting to maintain her poise, she said, 'What would you have done if I'd taken you up on your offer of hospitality?'

'Stood a lot of cold showers.' The admission was gritty but quite unapologetic. 'Every time I see you my most overriding impulse is to flatten you to the nearest horizontal surface. You probably made a wise decision.'

The insanity playing havoc with her senses lost its grip. The elastic snapped. Jake had always been able to stop at the wanting. Always. Leaning forward, her bitterness screened by a mocking smile, she pressed a playful set of fingertips to his shirt-front. 'Some time, Jake, I really must teach you how to make a sophisticated pass.'

A strong hand caught her fragile wrist, making her planned and immediate withdrawal impossible. 'Stop it,' he said very drily. 'Heaven Rothman goes down like a concrete block with me at any time of day. I'm not impressed.'

Voices from the kitchen were drifting up. Jake uttered a sharp imprecation and mercifully released her. She wanted to lift cool hands to her burning cheeks. He had shot her down in flames.

'Drew told me what happened. The minute I heard I came straight here. Is Tina in her room? I must go up and see her.' The breathless, husky voice was suddenly matched to an identity.

A tall, generously curved brunette with curly hair and long legs, flatteringly displayed by a short skirt, walked out of the kitchen into the hall. Bright blue eyes zoomed in on Kitty and narrowed to ice shards. 'This is Kitty, Paula,' Jake murmured.

Paula gave an affected laugh and barely touched the hand Kitty casually extended. 'I hardly needed to be told. I shouldn't think there's a soul in a hundred-mile radius who wouldn't recognise you after all the publicity you've had.' She laughed again, immediately switching her attention back to Jake. 'I must go up and check on Tina.'

His dark eyes rested consideringly on Paula's brightly smiling face. 'She's asleep. Kitty managed to settle her.'

Kitty's fingernails were biting painfully into her palm. Offended colour had raced into the other woman's complexion. She wasn't tanned, Kitty noted. His and hers matching tans would have turned her stomach over violently.

'I must be going.' She edged towards the kitchen, wishing she had parked at the front of the house.

'I'll see you out to your car,' Jake asserted.

'Is that old car out there yours?' Paula gasped in not very convincing surprise. 'Sorry, I hope you don't think I meant to be rude.'

'Now why would I think that?' Kitty parried gently, tired of the brunette's unsubtle barbs. The 'little girl' mode of gushing speech, employed by a female she suspected to be several years her senior, set her teeth on edge.

'I thought you might be stopping for lunch,' Jessie complained when she walked through the kitchen.

'I'll stay,' Paula interposed in a high, bright voice. 'It would be silly for me to go home again when we're off to Scarborough this afternoon.'

Jake strode ahead of Kitty and tugged open her car door. 'I didn't quite get around to it before, but I want to thank you for being so kind to Tina.'

She threw his dark, inhibiting presence a careless smile. 'I'd have done as much for any child.'

As she drove past the green saloon car parked beside the Range Rover, she was stabbed by a pang of guilty unease. Paula had every reason to be antagonistic. Paula knew that Jake and Kitty were not meeting with the harmless part indifference of former childhood friends. The other woman had made not the smallest attempt to disguise her hostility.

How long had Jake and Paula been together? Certainly long enough for Paula to walk into Torbeck with confidence and behave like a member of the family. She was extremely attractive. God, I hope thunder and lightning flash over Scarborough; I hope they get a flat tyre on the way home; I hope they have a rotten, lousy day together! Kitty pushed her hair off her damp brow, sickly dismayed by her vitriolic prayers.

Would Paula be staying while Mrs Tarrant was away? Someone had to be in the house at night for Tina. Who more natural than Paula? A tormenting vision of Jake's lean, brown body entwined with Paula's in the intimacies of passion provoked nauseous cramps in her stomach. Indeed, as she stumbled out of the car at Lower Ridge, she felt so sick she thought she might actually throw up.

It is none of your business. He made it my business. I didn't ask for this to start. For what to start? A few stolen kisses, a voice clarified drily. But no, it was more, so much more than that. How could she pretend otherwise? Even years ago on that one reckless night it had never been as it was now between them...explosive, savage. She could have wept when she thought of the men who had tried to overcome her reserve with persuasive charm and practised compliments.

Not once had she been tempted. Not once had the physical needs she had denied for so long made demands she couldn't cope with. But Jake dumped her on a heap of straw and she went crazy. He was the one man in the world she ought to be proof against. Instead she had behaved like the tramp he was so keen to make her out to be. But hadn't she exerted herself to give him exactly that impression? 'What do you want from me?' he had demanded rawly, revealing the first subtle shift in his attitude. Jake was starting to ask questions.

In some dark secret reach of her subconscious, had she returned to Yorkshire seeking a confrontation with Jake? And if she had, what was she doing now? Hurting all over again, hurting for pointless ifs and buts and what-might-have-beens that had only ever had substance in her own imagination. Jake had never loved her, and yet once she had been so confidently sure of that love even before he had voiced it. It was that thinking, that stubbornly wrong reasoning that had brought her life down around her in broken pieces.

Where was the hatred she had been convinced she felt for Jake? Had it ever been real hatred? Or an amalgam of bitter loss and pain? That hatred wasn't there now as a defence mechanism when she needed it. She had thought and reacted like a silly, emotional teenager ever since she had come back here.

Ties of childhood and a tragic first love were not so easily forgotten. A lovelorn adolescent seemed to be making her presence felt in these mixed up responses of hers. First love, that was all it had ever been. She liked the description. It took the steam out of her confused emotions, steadied her again. He attracted her still. That was all, absolutely all. And the problem was easily dealt with. Paula could keep her claws sheathed. Kitty would keep her distance.

The rain turned to sleet in the afternoon. Not the weather for a fun day out in Scarborough, she reflected, and was immediately annoyed with herself. The next morning she awoke to a white world, her body lethargic after a restless night. The bedroom was bitterly cold. Where was the old electric fire she remembered? The big cupboard in the corner went deep under the eaves. After she was dressed she explored the cupboard and found the fire tucked in a cardboard box. It needed a plug. She would fix it later. After breakfast she needed to go down to the village. Her fresh food supply had run out. And she wasn't in hiding, was she? Out of *The Rothmans* and no longer connected with Grant, she doubted that her whereabouts would be of interest to anybody.

She had driven about three miles when the engine developed an uneven chugging noise. The accelerator lost power and the car rolled to a dead halt in spite of her frantic efforts to revive it. She cursed. She wasn't dressed for a wintry trudge. Her flying suit was stylish but thin, and her raincoat no more sensible.

Her stiletto-heeled boots had no grip on the icy road surface. She had been slipping and sliding along the rough verge for about twenty minutes when she heard the approach of a car. Her sense of relief was short-lived when Jake's Range Rover stopped beside her. Her smile died.

Thrusting open the passenger door, he leant out. 'I saw your car back there. What happened?'

'I don't know but it sounded terminal,' she muttered thinly through chattering teeth.

He angled a rawly amused glance over her, taking in the tangle of her wind-whipped hair and the dirty splashes on her pale coat. 'Not exactly dressed for the weather, are you? I suppose you want a lift.'

Furiously aware of how ridiculous she looked, her quick temper surged. 'I don't. I'm perfectly capable of walking into the village on my own two feet,' she assured him, stuffing her frozen hands into her pockets and turning away.

'Don't be so bloody stupid,' Jake breathed impatiently. 'Get in and I'll run you to the garage.'

'No, thanks!' she slammed back fiercely at him. 'Why don't you mind your own business? Why can't you just stay out of my life?'

His charcoal gaze rested on her impassively. 'If that's what you want.'

He drove off. Kitty stared after the disappearing vehicle. For several seconds, she couldn't actually believe he had left her there. Icy snowflakes drifted down slowly on to her unprotected head. 'Yes, that's what I want,' she muttered, a little dazed by her own behaviour.

She had trudged another endless hundred yards when the Range Rover returned. The door fell open silently in front of her. Biting her lip painfully, she slid into the warm interior.

'I didn't want your body turning up after the thaw,' he said flatly.

'I shouldn't have lost my temper like that.' Every syllable hurt her bruised pride.

'Let's just concede that we both have a short fuse,' he dismissed.

That was it. That was the entire conversation until they reached the garage. She handed her keys over to a dour, middle-aged mechanic and he suggested that she phone him late afternoon. As Jake swung back into the Range Rover, the breeze raked his thick black hair back from his hard profile and something painful tightened a knot in her stomach, making it impossible for her to breathe. Tautly she looked away again.

'I've got some things to take care of at the surgery. I should be about an hour,' he delivered. 'If you can fill in the time, I'll give you a lift back.'

He dropped her outside the post office. The chatter of the women at the counter died on her entrance and only picked up again slowly while she loaded a wire basket. She was walking up the hill, laden with carrier bags when the screech of brakes tore up the quiet.

Tina mounted the pavement and hurled herself at her knees. A van had been forced to an emergency stop by the child's impetuous dash across the road. Through the windscreen the driver's face was a pale blur of fright. He pumped his horn angrily, belatedly, before driving on. Jessie appeared then, breathlessly shaking her head in mute shock.

Kitty bent down to Tina. 'You should always look to see if a car is coming, Tina. That car could have killed you.'

'I s'ought you'd gone away and then I saw you,' Tina mumbled tearfully. 'Now you're cross.'

'I was cross because you might have been hurt.' Tina looked up at her with drowning eyes and a shaky mouth. With a groan, Kitty gathered her into her arms. 'You mustn't ever do that again, Tina.'

'She'll be the death of me yet,' Jessie complained irritably.

'I need looked after. It's a lot of work,' Tina whispered guiltily in Kitty's ear.

Kitty told the older woman about her car. 'If he said an hour, he'll probably be two,' Jessie said confidently. 'This is my day off. You can come home and have a cup of tea with me.'

Five minutes later they walked into a small pin-neat terrace at the top of the hill. Jessie held out a hand for Kitty's coat, casting an impatient glance down at Tina, who was clinging possessively to a corner of the fabric.

Kitty gently detached the small hand. 'It's only because she's seen me on TV. I'm a novelty.'

Jessie sat the child down with a jigsaw in the lounge. 'You stay here while Kitty and I make the tea.'

'I wanna stay with Kitty,' Tina whispered.

Kitty's 'I won't be a minute,' was matched by Jessie's 'Do as you're told and no nonsense!'

Kitty was shown to a seat in Jessie's scrupulously tidy kitchen. 'Little pitchers have big ears,' she said meaningfully.

'Why do you have her on your day off?'

'Merrill's supposed to be keeping her, but she's got a hospital appointment today.'

'It must be awkward for you when Mrs Tarrant's away,' Kitty remarked.

'She didn't mean to smack Tina that hard, you know.' Jessie spoke abruptly. 'She's got no patience with her. She's not used to kiddies...had a nanny and boarding schools for her own, didn't she? She can't help the trouble she has with her nerves.'

Kitty nodded understandingly and Jessie's anxious look cleared. 'I don't mind her being away. A break at her sister's does her good.' She paused before continuing, 'She doesn't know that you're staying at Lower Ridge.'

Kitty shrugged. 'Why should she?'

'I would have said if Jake hadn't told me not to mention it. Funny, I thought.' Jessie's gimlet gaze, brimming with curiosity, rested on Kitty's perplexed face. 'What Miss Sophie doesn't like, she's always had to live with. Jake goes his own road.'

Tina sidled in and attempted to inch on to Kitty's lap.

'Can you not give Kitty peace?' Jessie scolded, and Tina fled in tears before Kitty could intervene. Jessie sighed. 'There's no sense in letting her get too attached to you. She's done nothing but talk about you since you brought her home.'

'Surely she's more attached to Paula?'

'Paula's not got your soft way with her.'

Unable to stand Tina's sobs from the next room, Kitty went through to pluck the child from the settee.

'See what I mean? Soft.' Jessie stared at her intently. 'Don't hurt him.'

'Hurt?' Jake, she was talking about Jake, Kitty registered in disbelief. Hurt Jake, she reflected incredulously as she sipped at her tea. Jake was invulnerable. She might annoy him, she might have made a few unwelcome ripples in his well-ordered existence, but that was the height of her influence.

Jessie had an air of stubborn purpose. 'I've known both of you since you were children,' she pronounced. 'I see what I see. There's a bond between you and there always will be.'

'Maybe...when we were very young. But it's a long time gone.' Lowering her head, Kitty was stabbed by a pang of painful regret for the child she had lost. That last bitter blow had concluded her obsession with Jake...hadn't it? Tina requested help with her jigsaw and provided a very welcome distraction from her uneasy thoughts.

Kitty only had to cross the road to the veterinary surgery. She followed the sound of voices coming from the waiting-room. The slim redhead in the doorway gasped, 'Kitty! I'd heard you were up here but I couldn't believe it! How long are you staying? For heaven's sake, don't you know me, Kitty?' Round blue eyes hardened with annoyance. 'We went to school together for years and years.'

Kitty smiled. 'Isabel.'

'Isabel Stevens that was. I'm a Hollister now.' Isabel preened herself on the announcement.

Kitty had to plumb her memory to recall that the Hollisters owned a chain of hotels on the Yorkshire coast.

'Look, we're having a big party tomorrow night. I'll absolutely die if you don't come,' Isabel gushed.

'I really don't think——'

'George and I throw terrific parties and we'd adore to have you,' Isabel interrupted insistently. 'But I simply can't stop to chat now. I'll see you tomorrow night, then. Dress formal, but I'm sure I don't need to tell you that these days.'

With a wave of a hand glittering with rings, Isabel and her cat-box surged out to the white Porsche parked outside on double-yellow lines.

'Isabel and hit-and-run drivers have a lot in common.' Drew Matcham strolled forward, grinning. 'I recognise that dazed look on your face. She has the same effect on me.'

Kitty laughed. 'You never could get a word in edgeways with her. Is Jake here?'

'He's outside. I'll give him a shout, shall I?'

From the window Kitty could see Jake and Paula standing talking in the rear car park. She shook her head. 'I can wait.'

'You really should go to the Hollisters' party. I'm going myself. On my own,' he admitted cheerfully. 'If you like...'

Kitty's attention was still helplessly pinned to the window. Paula's hand rested on Jake's sleeve, unconcealed urgency in her upturned face, an intrinsically feminine and yielding quality in the curve of her body into his. Kitty turned her head away sharply, swallowing back the sick fullness closing up her throat.

'I could pick you up at eight,' Drew was saying.

'Eight?' she echoed.

'For the party. No sense in both of us going solo,' Drew pointed out lightly. 'Well, what do you say?'

Kitty was seized by a sudden impulse. Her smile was blindingly bright. 'Why not?'

A phone rang and Drew grimaced as he went to answer it. Jake strode in. 'Sorry. Have you been here long?'

'A few minutes.' Kitty was unable to kill the defensive ice in her voice.

'My apologies, milady.' He was unconcerned by her tone; mockery gleamed in his assessing gaze.

Just outside the village he swerved to avoid a dog. The movement threw Kitty against him and she flung out a hand. It landed on lean, supple thigh. His muscles contracted to steel and she snatched her fingers away again, hot, burning awareness shock-waving through her tensed frame.

A desperate need to break the silence forced her into speech. 'Do you think the snow's here to stay?'

He flung his dark head back and laughed with rich appreciation, shooting her a brilliant glance of acute understanding. 'Why don't you talk about what you're thinking about? For a woman who freely admits that she enjoys making love, you're strangely reticent all of a sudden...' Heat flamed below her cheekbones. His animal-direct dark eyes issued an invitation that was rawly sexual, underplayed by the sardonic line of his sensual mouth. 'And oddly silent.'

'We've got nothing to talk about,' she snapped.

He drew up outside the cottage. 'At least, nothing that you could feel safe talking about,' he completed, lazily provocative.

CHAPTER FIVE

THE same clothes Kitty had brought from Los Angeles had travelled north with her. For the party, she selected a sapphire-blue and black Valentino that would have been a disaster on anyone with a less than perfect figure. It screamed expense and daring and Kitty donned it like a suit of armour, brushing her hair into a mass of burnished silk and dabbing Giorgio to her pulse-points.

The Hollisters lived in a split-level, ultra-modern house on the other side of the village. Isabel and her plump, balding little husband pounced on Kitty just inside the door. 'I've simply got to introduce you to everybody. What a ravishing dress! Valentino, isn't it? I'm into Saint Laurent this season.'

The party was an elegant crush, kept afloat on champagne and carefully selected mood music. Kitty was conscious of abrupt little silences and bursts of speech as she was carried deeper into the room by her determined hosts. She smiled and chatted until her jaw ached, radiating the scintillating allure that had enabled Heaven Rothman to steal every scene on camera.

In the end it backfired on her. She found herself circling the floor, gripped in an over-enthusiastic embrace by George Hollister. He had had too much to drink and her temper was sparking when Jake appeared out of nowhere and cut in. 'Excuse me, George.'

He swept her deftly out of the older man's grasp. 'Your hostess will soon be spitting tacks.'

'She ought to put a spiked collar and chain on him, but I could have coped without the rescue party,' Kitty said acidly.

'I'd noticed that Heaven was in the ascendant this evening. Drew doesn't know how to put a cap on a volcano. Where is he, by the way?'

She tore her hungry eyes from the dark splendour of his features and knew, knew with the bitter certainty of complete self-knowledge, that this moment was what she had been waiting for all evening. 'He's gone to get me a drink. I didn't see you earlier.'

'Paula and I were late arrivals. Tell me, do you usually dance a foot away from your partner?' A lean hand settled to her hip, urging her closer, forcing her hands up to his broad shoulders. It was a taste of heaven and hell in one go, the thin fabric of her gown no protection against the virile thrust of his hard thighs. A searing, irradiating heat sent a shaft of lust through her in a hot, ungovernable force that swept her with dizzying weakness. The pagan beat of hunger was in her veins, shattering all self-control, melding her to him in an anguish of desire.

The music ended and he severed her cruelly from the source of that unbearable need. She blinked rapidly, her pupils unfocused, her breath a feathery insufficiency to her lungs. Even so, sixth sense warned her that many eyes were watching them. With a sparkling smile she moved blindly away from him.

Isabel was waiting for her. 'Drew's been called out to some pedigree pig, of all things!' She giggled. 'He said he should be back in an hour. Poor Drew. Nothing ever goes right for him. He always pulls the short straw.'

'Does he?' Kitty wasn't listening. Paula, vibrant in scarlet that enhanced her lush, dark colouring, was dancing with Jake. Exuding animation, she wound her arms possessively round his neck and reached up to press her mouth briefly to his, flinging her head back again afterwards with an air of almost defiant triumph.

Kitty snatched a glass from a passing waiter's tray, the sick bile of jealousy like a thousand knives in her stomach.

'Drew's my cousin, you know.' Isabel leant confidentially closer. 'He's nuts about Paula but he doesn't have a chance at the moment. Paula's hunting for bigger game, and in her place I guess I would too. Jake is so incredibly sexy,' she savoured. 'All that brooding intensity matched to that don't-give-a-damn air and those stunning looks of his make him an irresistible challenge to our sex. Paula's no wiser than the rest of us.'

Kitty met Isabel's faintly malicious stare levelly. 'Jake and I are old friends.'

'If George had a friendship like that, I'd claw her eyes out. You leave Paula at the starting-line.' Isabel laughed. 'I could feel the heat from here, but then Jake prefers blondes. Liz was a blonde, small, rather like you at first glance.'

The words hung in the air and a tiny pulse flickered betrayal at the base of Kitty's throat. 'Really?'

Isabel studied her intently. 'Yes, it was the oddest marriage. She would have tied herself to the railway track for him but she couldn't handle that aloof quality of his. She tried to make him jealous and he didn't bat a magnificent eyelash. Women have been known to dash themselves to pieces against that brand of bedrock self-assurance. Jake is not a pussycat you stroke unwarily.'

Isabel's brother, Mike, crashed the one-sided conversation to ask Kitty to dance. She assented with relief and it was another hour before she was able to evade a constant stream of eager partners. She freshened up in a bathroom with grotesque gold dolphin taps, and on the way back to the party wandered into the cool, inviting depths of greenery in the conservatory off the hall.

The champagne had gone flat in her bloodstream. Her head felt dull, heavy. She practised an increasingly weary smile that meant nothing. Rather like you . . . rather like you. Her teeth clenched. Oh, sweet lord, was she never to be free of this ceaseless craving?

'God may have created woman . . .'

Kitty spun. Jake emerged from the shadowy tangle of jungle vines obscuring the door. 'But Maxwell created Kitty,' he concluded softly.

'Yes.' It was an answering taunt. 'He taught me how to walk, he taught me how to talk, he even taught me how to dress—— '

'Maxwell's little doll,' he incised pityingly.

'I don't think that's funny!'

He released his breath slowly. 'It's not funny, it's very sad. Do you enjoy yourself when you're acting your heart out? Of course, they're loving it in there. Larger than life is what the audience wanted and got, but I don't appreciate the show even if it was all put on for my benefit.'

'Your benefit?' she railed tempestuously.

He smiled at her slowly. 'Don't kid yourself, Kitty. Heaven could sink a knife into me and laugh but you'd lunge for the Band-aid,' he murmured. 'I think it's time we called a truce.'

Her mouth twitched against her volition. 'I wasn't aware we were fighting.'

He captured her easily with one powerful hand, his other catching a handful of hair that shimmered like a river of silver over his long fingers. The tawny glow of his eyes mesmerised her. 'You can't fight yourself, Kitty. You'll only tear yourself in two. And if you fight me, you'll lose, because I'll always be stronger than you are.' He lowered his head, the tip of his tongue tracing the tremulous curve of her lower lip with teasing provocation. 'I'll take you riding tomorrow afternoon. Heaven doesn't ride, does she?'

His mouth was a tantalising whisper from hers and she shivered violently. 'No.'

He released her. 'Thank God for that. Tell me, do you think George plays out his Tarzan fantasies in here on these vines?'

She burst out laughing.

'We really ought to go and look for our respective partners.' He gave her a wolfish grin and her world tilted on its axis.

Drew was in the hall, chatting to George. He spent the entire drive home apologising. 'Let me treat you to lunch on Friday,' he urged, and he had such a hangdog look that she agreed.

It took her forever to fall asleep, and when she did she had a dream filled with such explicit imagery that she awoke in a tangle of bedclothes, moist-skinned and shaken. She would have tied herself to a railway track for him. Kitty squeezed her eyes tight shut, racked by hatred of her own weakness. It was almost noon when she awoke again.

She had just finished lunch when her car was delivered back. The mechanic thrust her keys into her hands. 'It's running fine now, Miss Colgan. It wasn't a big job.'

'How much do I owe you?'

He looked at her in surprise. 'Jake Tarrant took care of that this morning.'

Her skin flamed. That would be a titbit to be savoured in the post office. How dared he do that? She stalked out to her car. A heavy night of rain had banished the snow and she drove over to Torbeck in record time.

Jake strode out of the stables, clad in a pair of tight, disreputable jeans and a shirt. 'I was going to pick you up in half an hour.'

'I'm not over here to go anywhere with you,' Kitty assured him vehemently. 'I'm only here to settle my garage bill.' She slapped her cheque-book down on the bonnet of her car. 'What do I owe you?'

He dug a brown hand carelessly into the pocket of his jeans. 'You can start with an apology.'

'An apology?' she mocked coldly.

'Hanvey won't release a car until the bill is paid. I saved you the hassle of going to the garage and you got your car back quicker. The receipt's still in the surgery and I can't recall the amount offhand,' he advanced curtly.

She put her cheque-book away. 'It seems I misunderstood.'

'Something you excel at.' He cast her a grim glance and disappeared back into the stables.

Kitty hesitated, reached for her car door and then hovered. She walked into the stables. 'I'm sorry.'

'Do you really have to seize on every excuse to pick an argument and keep me at a distance? Or is it just something you can't help?' he shot at her.

She moved forward, suddenly desperately uncertain of herself. 'I said I was sorry.'

He surveyed her reflectively and then straightened from the black mare he was saddling up. 'I should make you do this for yourself.'

'Jake, I can't stay,' she muttered.

He studied her with unyielding calm and she started to try and justify her announcement. 'I haven't got any boots.'

'Try the tack-room,' he advised gently.

'You're not any tidier than you used to be,' she called as she rustled through the dusty collection of riding boots, and all the time, I shouldn't be doing this, I shouldn't be doing this was racing through her brain.

'How long is it since you've been riding?'

She swallowed. 'Grant has a ranch in Texas. We usually go there in the spring.'

Jake led a big grey stallion out of the stable and swung gracefully up into the saddle. The little mare pranced skittishly and Kitty tightened the reins. 'What do you call her?'

'Misty.'

'Is she Merrill's?'

His firm mouth twisted. 'She sometimes rides her, but I bought her for Liz.'

Once they left the fields behind, Jake gave the stallion his head and Kitty followed suit, as confident in the saddle as he had taught her to be. Misty responded with an enthusiastic gallop which still failed to keep her anywhere near the powerful stallion. Out on the moor, Jake reined in and waited for them. 'It's going to rain. We should turn back.'

'No, I'm enjoying myself,' she protested.

'All right, we'll head for the Tor.' He indicated the overhanging rocks that had transformed the brow of the hill into a cliffside. 'We'll get some shelter there.'

'How's Tina doing?' she asked quietly.

'Yesterday she was down with a twenty-four-hour flu bug, but she's fine this morning,' he told her, interpreting her anxious glance.

'She's very... shy,' Kitty selected carefully.

He dealt her a perceptive scrutiny. 'Liz wasn't much of a mother. Once the novelty of a baby wore off, she found child-rearing a drag. Tina was only two when Liz walked out. It made her very insecure.'

Kitty's head was swimming. The assumption of years were taking a beating. 'Liz left you?'

'Liz was a spoilt and very demanding only child. When we married I was up to my eyes in work and responsibilities.' He sighed. 'I didn't have the time to give her the attention she wanted so she looked for it elsewhere. Her flirtations were intended to make me sit up and take more notice of her but I'm afraid I'm not one of Pavlov's dogs.'

Kitty bent her head. 'No,' she acknowledged.

He smiled grimly. 'I was twenty-three years old and I didn't have a lot of patience. There just wasn't enough of me to go round. Liz raved about the country life until she experienced the reality and then she wanted me to sell up and move. At the time I couldn't have afforded to do that. I worked an eighteen-hour day and I came home to hysterical scenes. At some stage I stopped listening to her. I switched off.'

'I don't think you can blame yourself for that,' she whispered ruefully.

His nostrils flared. 'Can't I? Liz lived on the periphery of my life and she knew it. Having Tina was a last-ditch attempt at a reconciliation. It didn't work,' he confessed harshly. 'Liz felt trapped by Tina and she had an affair. To tell you the truth, I didn't give a damn when I found her out.'

Kitty paled under the fierce challenge of his dark eyes as he continued, 'Sometimes I hated her for the way she treated Tina. When she left, she never once came back to visit her. Tina was devastated. I started divorce proceedings. Liz phoned me up in a passion to tell me that she was leaving the man she was with and coming back. She was heading for Torbeck when she crashed her car.'

'That wasn't your fault,' Kitty argued. 'It takes two to mess up a relationship.'

His golden gaze narrowed. 'It also takes two to make one work again.'

She evaded that look. Ominous drops of rain were dampening her cheeks. 'I think we need that shelter now fast,' she teased.

She reached the Tor a minute behind him. He lifted her down out of the saddle. 'Hell, you're soaked!' he grated angrily.

The rain lashed down a few feet away, streaming off the weathered canopy of rock above. She shivered in the clammy embrace of her thick wool sweater and blinked the moisture out of her eyes. Jake stripped off his weatherproof jacket. 'Take it off.'

'I've got nothing on underneath it!'

An earthy grin slashed his damp features and her heartbeat accelerated. 'I'm not about to offer to stand out in the rain.'

'It'll dry on me,' she muttered, folding her arms.

'Tease,' he whispered, draping his jacket round her shoulders.

'I think this is on for the day. There's no point in hanging on here.' Rounding breathlessly, Kitty was trapped in the circle of his arms. The stroking caress of his thumb laid her lips apart. 'Don't touch me,' she said jerkily. 'I hate it when you touch me.'

'God, what a liar you are,' he murmured appreciatively and the hot, hard seizure of his mouth annihilated her response with a savage demand that both tortured and triumphed over her. She went up in flames, heat burning between her thighs, her hands clinging to him, tugging him feverishly closer, wanting to be absorbed into his flesh.

A few feet away Misty snickered restively and Kitty reared back from him, wildeyed. He reached for her again. 'Relax.'

Kitty backed off. 'No! I won't let you do this to me!'

Mahogany eyes fastened on to her in an almost physical current. 'Do you ever intend to take responsibility for your own sexual urges? Or are you always going to be the victim of elements and circumstances nobody could possibly expect you to control for yourself?' he derided.

'I'm going home. I should never have come here,' she gasped strickenly.

The rain was slackening off and she vaulted back on to Misty in a surge of frantic energy. He would destroy her if she let him. Well, she wasn't about to let him do that to her again. Fearfully she repressed the knowledge that when he had talked to her about Liz out on the moor, she had felt the strengthening of bonds she had long denied, drawn forth by his blazing candour.

In the yard at Torbeck, she dismounted and headed straight for her car.

'Will you have dinner with me tonight?'

Arrested by the invitation, she swung round, trembling. Her lips framed an answer they didn't want to frame. 'No.'

The aggressive set of his jawline hardened. 'I won't ask you again.'

Kitty laughed but it didn't come out right. She was closer to tears. 'I just wanted you to ask me once.'

She crunched the gears driving off, and at the foot of the lane she crammed her knuckles against her wobbly mouth. Something she had wanted and dreamt about and been ready to die for eight years ago had finally been offered to her when it was too late.

Drew arrived promptly the next day to take her to lunch. She got ready in a mad scramble. She had completely forgotten about him. For twenty-four hours her thoughts had been scampering round like mice on a treadwheel, never reaching a destination, never resting for a moment.

The fire in the lowlit lounge of the Bardsley Inn put out a welcoming blaze. The barman brought over their drinks quickly. Drew grinned at her. 'That was snappy service. I'm sure it wasn't for my benefit.'

They had the bar to themselves. Kitty stretched out her legs and slowly sank lower in her comfortable wing-chair. Drew's easy banter unwound her tightened nerves. When a burst of voices announced new arrivals, he lifted a hand in acknowledgement of whoever had entered and continued talking.

'Not quite your usual lunchtime haunt, Drew.' It was unmistakably Jake's husky drawl, mocking in tone. Kitty's hand jerked in reflex response. She almost spilt her drink.

Jake saw her at the last possible moment. The high-backed chair had hidden her from view. His hard-boned features clenched, his eyes narrowing to glittering shards. He held on to his smile with difficulty.

'It makes for a change.' Drew laughed, seemingly impervious to the sardonic twist of Jake's mouth. 'And, given the company and the weather, I'm feeling pretty pleased with myself.'

'Drew's been telling me some very funny stories.' Maintaining her attitude of total relaxation, Kitty treated Jake to a languorous smile.

He looked spectacular in a fine dark tailored suit, one hand thrust in the pocket of well-cut trousers that accentuated his narrow hips and long, lean thighs. He ignored her conversational opener. His hooded gaze smouldered down the length of her carelessly extended body. Wicked little tongues of flame scorched wherever his dark intent scrutiny lingered. Her mouth ran dry. He couldn't control that need to stare. He sent her a single electrifying glance of damped-down fury, his eyes damning her to hell and back for the effect she was having on him.

Only at that point did she consciously appreciate what she was doing. She drained her drink in one gulp, shamed by the recognition of her own instinctively provocative behaviour. With one glance she could freeze a polar bear at sixty paces, but when Jake looked at her she burned.

'I'll leave you to it, then,' Jake drawled softly. He strode down the room and joined two older men at a table.

'I see he's not with Paula,' Drew commented.

'Did you think he would be?' Kitty prompted. 'Is that why you brought me here today?'

His pleasant features were drenched by a slow tide of colour. Her curiosity satisfied, Kitty decided to let him off the hook. 'Have they been together long?'

He studied his glass. The pink was only retreating from the tips of his ears. 'Paula only moved up here last autumn. She had just come through a rather messy divorce. At the time I didn't think she was looking for a serious involvement, but I suspect her feelings have changed,' he said more evenly. 'And I don't believe that Jake's even aware that Paula's in the same room when you're in his vicinity. She would be better off without him.'

The owner of the inn intervened at that point to tell them that their table was ready. Drew didn't refer to Paula again. They were at the coffee stage when an American woman with an embarrassed husband in tow stopped by their table to demand an autograph.

'Have you and Grant really split up?' she gushed in decibels that echoed round the suddenly silent dining-room. 'I hope you get back together again, I really do. You always seemed so marvellously well suited to each other.'

As the woman reluctantly took her leave, Drew grimaced. 'I take back what I said about envying celebrity status. I noticed her staring at you but I didn't think she'd do anything about it.'

Faint flags of pink had burnished Kitty's skin. 'I'm used to it. It goes with the territory.'

As they walked out to his car, he said, 'Damn, I have a call to make at the estate. Do you mind if I make it now?'

She shook her head. On the outskirts of the village, Drew turned between stone pillars topped by weather-beaten lions. The rambling sprawl of Haggerston Grange was visible from the first bend in the driveway. The earliest part of the house was Georgian, but in Victorian times a wealthy Tarrant with a love of extravaganza had done his best to conceal that fact. Turreted wings, adorned by gothic windows and half shrouded by ivy rose at either end of the main building, were linked by a castellated frontage.

Drew made a sharp turn off the driveway into a lane. The old gatehouse had become the estate office. As he parked, she said, 'Do you think Mr Creighton would mind my having a look round the Grange? I'd love to see it again, and since it's empty...'

'Why not? I wouldn't object to having a tour either,' he confided, dismaying her. 'I shouldn't be long with Bob. He queries every bill we send him as a matter of course. I could follow you up there after we're finished.'

She hadn't wanted company, but she concealed her disappointment. Her impulsive suggestion hadn't allowed for the small amount of time at her disposal if Drew was not to be kept waiting for her.

The manager was a heavy-set man in his forties. He engulfed her hand in a hearty handshake. He would have kept her in conversation had not Drew helpfully intimated her desire to see the Grange.

Bob Creighton shot her a surprised glance. 'There's not a lot to see. It's a great barn of a place and it's not furnished, you know. The last tenant found the upkeep too hefty, but of course you're welcome to the keys.'

The consequences of the secrecy she had insisted on caused her colour to fluctuate. It didn't seem right to deal with this man without admitting that she was, in fact, his employer.

An estate worker escorted her up the lane. After warning her to watch out for loose floorboards, he cheerfully left her to her own explorations. The shabby exterior paintwork had made a bad first impression on her and the interior was no brighter. The elaborate plasterwork on the ceilings was dingy. Oak panelling was warped and discoloured by damp in the hall and the dining-room. As she wandered from room to room, she noted that the same signs of neglect and deterioration were everywhere.

Had the house been this run-down eight years ago? Her troubled eyes were rueful. To her then, this house had been the last word in absolute luxury. Antique furniture and Sophie Tarrant's decorative flair had undoubtedly concealed a wealth of flaws. Kitty was no longer surprised that the estate was having trouble in attracting a new tenant. The Grange required extensive renovation.

Well, maybe not that extensive, she adjusted thoughtfully. The panelling would be easily replaced. Bright, fresh colour would banish the shadows. She smiled, seeing the shutters thrown back in the drawing-room. The daylight would flood in again. She would drape the windows with gorgeous fabric, spread a rich Persian rug, and from that it was only a step to picturing the furniture.

But the floorboards echoed with her footsteps in the eerie silence. Bemusedly she shook her head as if to clear it of the fantasy that had seized a powerful hold on her imagination. She mounted the stairs to the second floor where Jessie's flat had been. Without conscious thought, she strolled into the room with the sloping ceiling where she had slept what now seemed a lifetime ago.

From the window she stared down unseeingly at the courtyard below. Jumping out of bed that morning, she had drawn a heart on the condensation on the pane. Kitty loves Jake, she had inscribed before sheepishly rubbing it out again. Distractedly her forefinger traced that former path on the dirty glass, as if she could feel again what she had felt then when she had still been more child than woman and in no way prepared for what was to come.

And was it that dreaming teenager or the adult she was now who controlled her emotions? A chill ran over her. She shivered and crossed her arms over her breasts to contain the sheer force of her fear. Could she still love Jake? Could God be so cruel? Could she still be so pitifully stupid? She thought of a tarnished silver trinket that she had never been able to bring herself to discard and the last veil of self-deception was ripped away. As answers came hammering back at her, she twisted clumsily and practically ran out of the room.

On the landing outside she froze in an attitude of flight, stricken paralysis seizing up her limbs. Jake was lounging against the wall a flight of stairs below her, dark animal-direct eyes nailed to her. A curious satisfaction dwelt in that unremitting stare.

CHAPTER SIX

'I KNEW you'd visit the scene of the crime.'

A headless ghost rattling spectral chains could not have shocked Kitty more. Mortification was eating her alive. Her heart jumping behind her breastbone, she stared mutely down at Jake, not entirely sure in her chaotic frame of mind that he *was* real.

'I see this is one of those rare occasions when you're stuck for a venomous come-back. Now, if I was a gentleman I wouldn't take advantage of that,' he murmured, settling a purposeful hand to the dusty bannister as he prepared to close the distance between them. 'But I don't feel like a gentleman——'

'Stay away from me!' Shrilly she recovered her tongue, a sixth-sense apprehension that had nothing to do with reasoning taking her over.

He mounted three steps with dark, prowling ease. 'You sound almost hysterical, Kitty.'

'Drew must be wondering where I am,' she muttered, fingering an unsteady hand through her hair.

'I'm afraid not. He left about ten minutes ago. I assured him that you'd reach home safely,' Jake imparted smoothly.

'You told him to leave and he just went?' She quivered with incredulous resentment.

'Admittedly it took a little persuasion, but Drew can take a hint like any other man even when he doesn't want to.' He took another lazy step up, a predator already confidently viewing a prey caught in a trap.

'What the heck did you think you were playing at?' she demanded, struggling to stand her ground when every nerve-ending was cravenly urging retreat.

'Kitty...the subtle difference between us is that I'm not playing.'

Her hands clenched by her sides. 'What are you doing here?'

A black brow arched. 'Looking for you, what else? I went to Lower Ridge first and then I came here. If I hadn't found you here, I'd have checked out every possibility until I ran you to ground,' he admitted. 'In short, I was determined that we would have this meeting.'

'Well, I don't want it...I don't want anything to do with you!' she flared.

'Then it seems to me that you've backed yourself into a tight corner. No audience and no rescue party,' he enumerated hardly. 'I can assure you that you're not leaving until I've finished with you.'

'If you dare lay a single finger on me——' she warned shakily.

'I plan to lay all ten on you before the day's out, and let's not deceive ourselves that that is a threat of violence.' The fading light issuing through the great, domed skylight above cast a shadowy darkness on the hard, angular planes of his sculpted features as he drew lithely level with her.

'I don't find that amusing!' His disturbing proximity made her step back a pace. She was as shamefully afraid of him as she was of herself. Her emotions were primed to fever pitch. She didn't trust her tongue, she didn't trust her mind and she didn't trust her body either.

'I wasn't joking.' Eyes topaz-bright between black luxuriant lashes held hers in glancing, remorseless challenge. 'And don't use Drew to strike back at me. I can take whatever you want to throw, but leave him out of it!' he gritted.

'I'm not using Drew for anything,' she countered angrily. 'But I don't need to explain myself to you. My God, you are so egotistical!'

'Am I?' he spoke caustically, contemptuously. 'You don't want Drew.'

She forced a laugh. 'I don't want you either, if that's what you're driving at. Now will you get out of my way? I intend to walk home.' Her voice pitch had acquired a thready tremor she despised.

He stayed exactly where he was, big and dark and very, very sure of himself. Raising a hand, he ran a taunting fingertip in a tormentingly slow trail over the warmth flooding her cheekbones. 'Where does the Amazonian stature go when we're alone?'

'Don't touch me!' Breathlessly she jerked her head back before that torturingly familiar weakness could seize hold of her defences. His tie was loose, the top two buttons of his shirt undone, framing a triangle of tawny skin. This close, the thin white silk was an insufficient barrier to conceal the dark whorls of hair hazing his chest. His hand had dropped down to rest on her shoulder and she knew an insane need to touch him and to match and deepen that contact. Her fingers braced on the door-frame behind her, seeking the strength not to sway forward, not in any way to invite or incite the smallest intimacy.

His thumb gently massaged the sensitive flesh just below her ear and her bones turned to water. 'No,' she muttered feverishly.

'Your game got out of hand, didn't it?' His dark skin bore the merest sheen of dampness, his eyes a merciless beat of gold on her strained face.

'There was no game!' she snapped starkly.

He wasn't listening to her. 'You're as caught up in this as I am, and I was never into spectator sports. I'm not into hole-in-the-corner affairs either.'

Her head flew back, strands of shimmering hair springing back from her slanted cheekbones in pale silk wings. 'I wouldn't have an affair with you if you were the last man alive on this earth!' she derided.

Long fingers were twining with caressing cool into her tumbled hair, smoothly preventing her from an inch of withdrawal. 'Well, that's what I came here to tell you, Kitty. As far as you're concerned while you're up here, I am the last man alive on this earth. I don't share,' he spelt out sibilantly. 'I don't care how you behaved with Maxwell, but by God you'll be different with me.'

An overriding awareness of the hand lazily tracing the line of her extended throat was turning her brain into an inactive wasteland. 'You're crazy!'

His mouth twisted. 'Ground rules not to my lady's fancy? They're on a take-it-or-leave-it basis. Non-negotiable,' he emphasised, his formerly even intonation steadily harshening. 'I'm not down on my knees, Kitty, and I never will be. So if that is your objective, you're in for a disappointment.'

The instant she attempted to jerk free, something seemed to snap in him. His eyes blazing down at her, he pressed her back against the wall. He took her lips fiercely, ravishing the tender interior of her mouth with his tongue until the hot blood pounded in her veins, sapping her of all will to protest. He trembled against her. With every lean line of his taut body moulded to her, she could not have been unaware of the extent of his arousal, yet she dimly sensed the duality in him, the anger as powerful as the hunger he couldn't deny.

He released her mouth with a ragged groan. 'God, not here...anywhere but here.'

Self-loathing dug bitter claws of reproach into her. She pulled violently free of his loosened embrace and made for the stairs. Near the foot of the first flight, her heel went skidding off the edge of a step, catapulting

her into the air. She landed with a sharp cry on hard
boards, her ankle twisted painfully beneath her. Hot tears
flooded and blurred her vision.

'You could have broken your neck!' He let rip at her
with a rage that made her flinch as he came down beside
her on his knees, careless of his suit. Firm hands pushed
away her clutching fingers and lightly probed her ankle.
'I imagine that hurt.' White under his tan, he stared down
at her, releasing his breath in a tortured hiss, none of
that anger betrayed by the gentle investigation he
pursued.

The tears she had been fighting inexplicably fell all
the more freely. 'Go away!' she sobbed furiously.

Instead he lifted her into his arms, cradling her against
his thighs as he sank back on the stairs, holding her as
easily as if she were a small child. Her hand balled into
a weak fist and struck against a broad, muscular
shoulder. 'Don't!' she gasped.

He pressed her hot face almost roughly into his shirt-
front. The throb of her ankle was already receding under
the soothing massage of his fingers. She struggled
hoarsely to catch her breath. The husky male scent of
his warm flesh was drowning her already stormed
defences. She felt weak and defeated, utterly incapable
of contesting the ridiculous sense of security she was
experiencing. His heart was a solid, reassuring thump
against her ear. He held her until her breathing steadied
and unwillingly she lifted her head away, her hair
screening her face from him.

'Do you miss this place?' she whispered in the strangely
comfortable silence.

Fingertips lightly caught her chin, pushing it up. 'What
do you think?' A ruefully amused smile played over his
mouth, softening the implacability so often etched there.
Her pulses quickened to the inherent dark charm of that
almost forgotten smile. 'Two hundred years of family

heritage once belonged under this roof. I knew when my father died that I'd never be able to keep it, but it didn't make moving out any easier.'

Her lashes cloaked her disquiet. Becoming uneasily conscious of the childish fashion in which she was still sprawled across his thighs, she slid on to the step beside him. 'Was there no way you could have kept the house?'

'At the time I couldn't afford the maintenance. A clean break seemed wisest,' he said dispassionately, his honesty piercing her with guilty discomfiture. 'Look around you. If certain steps aren't taken soon, this house will be derelict in another few years.'

'For goodness' sake, it's not that bad!' she protested.

'You'd be surprised how fast a house goes downhill when it's empty. The damp's getting in all over the place. The roof and the windows are overdue for renewal, and that would only be the beginning. I doubt if the consortium who owns the estate now would consider the expense worthwhile,' he drawled. 'It's hardly in the stately home bracket.'

'It's a very attractive house. It's unusual,' she argued half under her breath, constrained by the weight of her deception.

Jake grimaced. 'It's a Victorian folly, built for a half-dozen servants, not for convenience. It's surprising that the estate hasn't made more profitable use of it. It could be split up into apartments or even turned into a small hotel.'

Since both of his suggestions had been tabled to her and costed several years previously, she couldn't bring herself to look at him. At her insistence the Grange had remained a private dwelling. She swallowed. 'The condition of the house bothers you, doesn't it?'

'Possibly because there's always that little doubt that asks me if I tried hard enough to hang on to it,' he confessed bleakly as he slid fluidly upright and dusted himself down. 'How's your ankle? Can you stand?'

Clutching his supportive arm, she slipped back into her discarded shoe and tested her foot. 'It's fine,' she dismissed, immediately moving away from him. 'We should be going. Mr Creighton will be sending out a search party soon.'

He caught her hand, dark eyes diamond-hard on her withdrawn profile. 'You started this, you can't stop it now.'

'Tell me, where does Paula fit into this *ménage à trois*?' she prompted curtly.

'She doesn't. Paula and I had a convenient arrangement which is now at an end,' he breathed harshly. 'Paula appreciates her freedom as much as I do. I haven't even known her for very long. We have never been lovers, Kitty. If you are looking for an exit, you are not going to find it through Paula.'

She turned away, a prey to conflicting emotions. Guilt, relief, panic and pleasure all tore at her simultaneously. The emptiness of her unsteady hands provided a welcome distraction. 'I must have left my bag upstairs.'

He released his breath in the tension that had sprung up again. 'I'll get it.'

Momentarily she let her shoulders slump back against the wall. Dear God, what was happening to her? Ten minutes ago she had broken down completely and somehow Jake had put her together again. Eight years ago she had sewn up her emotions tight and now feelings that she had suppressed for so long were gushing out in a damburst. She was conscious of a treacherous, unreasoning happiness blossoming inside her.

He was hers. His violent pride might take refuge in aggression, but he was no more in control of events than she was. Even as she stood there, that bold belief faded, leaving behind an appalled awareness of her own vulnerability. He wanted no more from her than he had wanted before. What a fool she was, what a blind, stupid fool to still want him no less even facing that unpalatable fact!

Her feelings for Jake had limpet-strong tenacity. Breaking away would be like walking down these stairs. One step, then another, each one slightly harder, that invisible elastic fighting to yank her back to him, regardless of every self-preservative instinct. She remembered the dark days when despair had been her shroud, shutting out the rest of the world. Love was a gift, God's greatest gift, she had been taught in Sunday school. But love could be a burden and an agony, a ceaseless craving that you could be desperate to root out of yourself. And the will to do that seemed to be beyond her.

So she was always at the mercy of elements outside her control? No, she wasn't, she told herself fiercely. She would conclude this insanity before it went any further, and to reinforce that necessity she reminded herself painfully of the baby she had wanted to bring into the world in spite of his wishes. Then she had been infinitely less desirable. Jake had wanted neither her nor any child she might have been carrying. It was some minutes before she registered that Jake was taking a long time to join her.

'Jake!' Her call echoed hollowly in the dark hall.

She heard his steps a moment later. He strode down to her and tossed the bag casually into her hands. 'I'd forgotten what the view was like up there.'

The dark flush along his cheekbones, the rawness of his voice told its own story. There was no view to admire from that room. He was as over-sensitive to their surroundings as she had been.

'I want to talk to you about what happened then,' he imparted tautly.

'What is there to talk about?' There were years of training in the deprecating movement of her slim shoulder. 'We both made a mistake.'

His jawline clenched hard. 'It wasn't a mistake on my part.'

'At least you've become that honest with the passage of time.'

'Damn you, Kitty,' he said savagely. 'You're deliberately twisting my words.'

'Possibly because I don't want to discuss pre-history. The prospect makes me feel slightly tacky,' she replied coldly.

Dark eyes rested on her inscrutably. 'When you feel the need to shoot these world-weary lines, you really ought to aim them at someone who didn't know you when you were a child.'

Her colour heightened. She swung on her heel, her knees maddeningly wobbly. 'It's almost dark, Jake, and I'm tired.'

'Until I tell you why I married Liz, what happened eight years ago will still lie between us,' he bit out impatiently. 'Now are you going to make this easy or are you determined to make it difficult?'

She turned back to him. A band of steel tension was enclosing her pounding temples. 'I'm a dinosaur where forgiveness is concerned,' she whispered tightly. 'I've only got one question for you. Did you ever love her?'

Hooded dark eyes held hers unflinchingly. 'No.'

He hadn't lied and she was weak enough still to wish he had. She wasn't vain. He could easily have fallen in love with a more outgoing and mature girl than she had been then. 'So you got what you deserved,' she condemned very low.

'Liz got what I deserved,' he contradicted harshly. 'I should never have married her.'

A stifled laugh fell from her lips. 'I don't know, Jake. From where I stand you made a pretty cut-and-dried decision. You saw a chance and you took it and there was no way you were going to let me get in your path.'

His lean features hardened. 'Exactly what are you saying?'

'If you didn't marry her for love, you married her for money, and if it didn't work out too well, you've only got yourself to thank for it,' she said bitterly.

'Is that what you believe?' Although the demand was ominously quiet, the icy rage in his stare struck out at her in a chilling blast. He gazed at her with generations of bred-in-the-bone hauteur. 'Of course I should make allowances for you, Kitty. Selling yourself at nineteen to the highest bidder wasn't evidence of a more delicate frame of mind. Maxwell doesn't appear to have done much to raise the tone of those mercenary little brain cells.'

'How dare you talk to me like that?'

His dark head spun to the ajar front door. 'I heard a car.'

She swept past him, shaking with indignation. Bob Creighton appeared in the path of his car headlights and treated them both to a speculative scrutiny.

'I didn't realise you were still up here until I saw the car. Don't worry, I'll lock up.' The amused grin on his florid face brought heat to Kitty's skin even in the icy air.

She thanked him woodenly. 'Any time, Miss Colgan,' he breezed as she stepped into Jake's car.

Jake took his time about joining her. Indifferent to the cold, he lingered in the scant shelter of the porticoed entrance. Their gruelling exchange of words had left her raw and shaking. Jake, on the other hand, was coolly capable of trading casual conversation with the estate manager. Had he been attempting to deny her accusation? Or insidiously suggesting that at heart there was very little difference between them? His opinion of her was no higher.

When he swung in beside her, she couldn't help saying tartly, 'What was he grinning at?'

'Take your choice. It was either the movie queen exit or he was wondering what we were doing in the dark. I wouldn't be too hard on him,' he drawled. 'His suspicions weren't too far off beam.'

She pressed a moist palm to her throbbing brow. 'I don't want people talking about us——'

'There has to be an us to talk about,' he cut in coldly. 'And I really don't think that there is.'

Illogically, that hurt. It was what she ought to want to hear, what her sane mind wanted to tell him. Any relationship between them now would be utter madness. Yet still it hurt. She felt as if once again she had been tried and found wanting. His withdrawal filled her with a demeaning sense of rejection and a panicky sense of loss. Yet she had brought it on herself. she knew that. A sharp pang of anguish currented through her, wounding wherever it touched.

He drew up outside the cottage, his dark features impassive. 'It's going to snow again and you could well be drifted in up here. I assume you're well stocked up with food and fuel?'

'I can look after myself.'

'If you need help, ask for it. I can't see you defrosting frozen pipes in your four-inch heels and your designer raincoat,' he said drily.

Kitty couldn't get out of the car quickly enough. 'I can manage.'

'I wish I could believe that, but your track record for managing by yourself hasn't been too good in the last eight years,' he countered bleakly.

She slammed into the cottage. Behind the door her whole body slumped. She stumbled through to the scullery to dissolve a couple of pain-killers. Her headache abated steadily. An hour later she built up the fire again and sat down at her typewriter with driven resolution. What had she achieved in two weeks? One miserable chapter. The next opened on a blazing row between two complete strangers and she was just in the mood to attack that difficult scene with the spirit it required.

Late evening, she massaged her aching spine and surveyed the fat pile of manuscript paper with dulled satisfaction. She was in the bath when the insistent ring of the phone penetrated her thoughts. A frantic rush to answer it earned her only the frustrating click as the caller rang off. You thought it might be him, you flew down those stairs. Her own weakness tortured her.

Lying in bed with the radio for company, she reached a decision she would have been prouder to have reached a week ago. She would leave tomorrow. She would sell Lower Ridge. She would even sell the estate. There would be no ties left here then and no excuse ever to return. She had stopped bolstering up her pride with empty pretences.

The choices Jake had made at twenty-two had not killed her love for him. For too long she had sheathed her emotions in a forcing house of bitterness. And now the walls of her castle were falling down. Her black and white view of the past had blurred into disturbing grey shades.

An adoring and willing teenage girl could be an overpowering temptation to a virile young man. Jake had not deliberately set out to use and discard her. Fate had given them opportunity and mutual attraction had plunged them both into what followed. Afterwards, Jake had made an astonishingly clumsy attempt to deal with the situation, but ravaged by his conscience he had been out of his depth.

Had he already been planning on a rich wife? Jake had a bone-deep strength that could be uncommonly hard, and strength was frequently partnered by a composite degree of ruthlessness. He had always been fiercely loyal to his family. He had filled the gaps that his father had refused to fill. Even at seventeen Kitty had recognised his instinctive protectiveness towards his mother while she had fought to maintain a long-dead marriage. When the crash came, his sisters and his mother must have clung to him like drowning swimmers. Dear God, did she now start to excuse him for marrying Liz to rescue the family fortunes?

Kitty tasted the full force of her own weakness. If there was a defence to be made for Jake, she was pathetically keen to build up the case. A faint creak somewhere beyond the bedroom lifted her head. Frowning, she turned down the radio. When the door swung wide without any warning whatsoever, her heart leapt into her mouth. There was a split second of terror before she realised incredulously that it was Jake surveying her from the threshold.

'I did knock but you can't have heard me above the music. The front door's on the latch. You don't take many precautions for your own safety,' he censured. 'I'm not about to apologise for giving you a fright. I could have been anybody!'

'I forgot to lock up.' She was having difficulty breathing, never mind thinking. It was after midnight. What did he want, for goodness' sake?

His tailored suit had been replaced by a pair of tight-fitting black jeans that hugged his perfectly proportioned male physique with disturbing fidelity. The collar of his dark green weatherproof jacket was turned up. Melting snowflakes lent a crystalline shimmer to the black luxuriance of his hair.

He looked devastatingly dark and smoulderingly sexy, and as that unsought awareness occurred to her she was shaken afresh by her own shameless susceptibility. His keen gaze roamed boldly over her lace-edged sheets and pillowcases, glided over the ridiculous mound of quilts piled on top of the blankets for extra warmth, and lingered finally on the incongruity of the woolly shawl covering what little was visible of her.

'It's a little like the princess and the pea in reverse,' he quipped, strolling lazily forward, apparently impervious to her electrified tension. 'I certainly don't need to ask if you're feeling the cold.'

'Would you mind telling me what you're doing here?' She had intended to sound scornful but her treacherous voice emerged thin and shrill.

The glow of the lamp revealed a haggard tinge to his complexion. His wine-dark eyes had a reckless glitter, but the tense slant of his expressive mouth belied his air of slumbrous relaxation. He withdrew a bottle from one laden pocket and deposited it on the bedside cabinet. From his other pocket he produced a pair of twisted-stem, etched champagne goblets which gleamed with the fragile beauty of old glass. He slotted them neatly into her unprepared hands.

'Jake, I . . . what am I supposed to do with these?'

'I am trying to make an occasion of this.' Repossessing the bottle he sank down calmly on the side of the bed and flourished a corkscrew.

She clutched stupidly at the glasses. 'An occasion?'

'Maybe you do this all the time. I don't,' he extended flatly. 'And no, I wasn't trying to insult you——'

'You don't need to try, you're doing just fine!' she gulped, twisting abruptly to put the goblets down. Only a man would have pulled two such exquisite items out of an unprotected pocket with no more respect than he would have employed with a pair of tumblers.

His well-shaped dark head was bent, his chiselled profile turned to her. 'It might help if you stopped cringing and cowering back against the pillows like some pantomime Victorian virgin facing a violent intruder. My sense of humour isn't what it usually is tonight,' he confided.

CHAPTER SEVEN

BOTH incensed and mortified by the scathing description, Kitty gaped at Jake. Fortunately he wasn't looking at her. He was having a battle royal with the champagne cork. His lean hands were ever so slightly lacking in their usual dexterity. A pang of treacherous tenderness stole through her twanging emotional disarray. He couldn't stay; he couldn't possibly stay. He just couldn't walk in here when he felt like it, sling a bottle of vintage bubbly at her and expect to share her bed for the night. But that's what he's doing, a little voice screeched.

'Why are you here?' she probed breathlessly. 'I thought—— '

'Thinking's dangerous. Where we are concerned, it ought to be outlawed altogether. I should know.' Rising with the bottle, he let champagne froth into the waiting glasses. Black-lashed tawny eyes nailed themselves to her flushed face with inherent sensuality and her pulses started to race, her stomach turning over in a crazy little somersault. 'I could give you a dozen reasons why, but they all melt down to the same ego-zapping bottom line. I couldn't stay away,' he confessed with harsh sincerity. 'I also had the feeling that you might be contemplating doing a runner on me.'

Her tongue slunk out to moisten her dry lower lip. 'A runner?'

He slid a goblet between her nerveless fingers. 'You ran away from here once. You ran back here from

Maxwell,' he specified. 'But you're not about to do the same to me. I'm not giving you that amount of space.'

The golden obduracy of his eyes held her in mesmerised thrall. A mouse waking up to find the cat's paw firmly placed on its twitching tail could not have been more paralysed. 'It's cold up here,' she said abruptly. 'We'd be more comfortable downstairs. We could talk——'

'Talk?' His laugh was richly appreciative and yet somehow embittered as well. 'You want to talk about eight years that neither of us wants to live with? It was rather naïve of me to imagine that we could talk. In any case, I'm not cold, Kitty.' A brilliant smile lifted the hardness from his expressive mouth. 'And I promise that you won't be either.'

Shrugging gracefully out of his jacket, he cast it carelessly across the footboard before lifting his own glass. Stalled in her clumsy attempt to defuse an explosive situation, she unwittingly twirled her glass back and forward, forward and back between her fingers in a revealing metronome of her inner perturbation. She wanted the impossible. She wanted to send him away but she wanted him to come back. With hindsight that was cold comfort now, she saw how provocative her behaviour must have seemed to him.

Would he credit that that had been neither conscious nor deliberate? Would he not be more inclined to believe that her present reluctance was another unpleasant step in some despicable game? She snatched a sip of champagne, dying bubbles tickling her throat. With a casual yank of a hand, he displaced the abundance of quilts and cast them on to a nearby chair where they promptly spilled to the floor.

He studied her tense stillness in the bed quizzically. 'I could be forgiven for suspecting that now that you've got me you don't quite know what to do with me,' he murmured softly. 'Isn't that a crazy idea?'

She tried and failed to laugh, her eyes mirroring her confusion. 'Did you try to phone earlier?'

'No. It wasn't me. I was too busy driving fifty miles in pursuit of a presentable bottle of champagne. I really don't know why I bothered.' His intent gaze rested on her with a sudden flash of savage, undisguised hunger and she felt as if she had gone down in a lift too fast, her breathing quickening, her stomach clenching. 'Now that I'm here, I don't even want to drink it. I don't want to think about tomorrow or the next day either. I just want you . . . or as much of you as I can have,' he completed in a husky growl.

'I can understand how things might have seemed to you, but I'm really not in the habit of leaping into——' a brown hand deftly deprived her of her glass and tripped her into startled repetition '——leaping into bed with men.'

'I hope not in the plural sense.' It was a mocking intercession. 'And you don't have to leap anywhere, Kitty. You're exactly where I want you to be.'

Sinking down on the bed again, he leant forward. His hands braced on the pillow on either side of her face, his warm breath fanning her cheek. He slowly circled her damp lips with the tip of his tongue, delving expertly between to tease her and taste her until her senses swam with dizziness and she had to put her hands up to his broad shoulders to convince herself that she was still on solid earth.

'Jake,' she mumbled dazedly.

'You can't possibly be shy with me.' His fingers sensuously cradled the nape of her neck, and this time he kissed her with a shockingly sexual urgency that drained her woolly brain of rational thought for endless minutes.

She opened her eyes and he was undressing, peeling off his shirt to reveal the smattering of black, curling hair that sprinkled his well-muscled chest and arrowed down in an intriguingly silky furrow over his flat belly to disappear tantalisingly beneath his low-slung belt. Her moral principles took her to the door on a hurried exit...but her body stayed where it was on the bed, strangely weighted and unmoving. She was spellbound by his masculine beauty. Tawny skin blended perfectly over sleek, strong bones and whipcord muscles. Words like spectacular and gorgeous seethed in her chaotic thoughts, embarrassing her into tearing her attention from him. Sanity made one last attempt to be heard. 'This isn't sensible.'

'I'm feeling many things at this moment,' he admitted. 'Sensible isn't one of them.'

Her heart was beating so fast it scared her. The mattress depressed again with his weight. Just this once, just this once, she bargained wildly with herself, and she knew even then that she was lying. She was hooked on Jake and he was a dangerous addiction. Time had only deepened her dependency.

He drew her slowly into the heat of his embrace, pressing his lips to a sensitive spot just below her ear. Her entire body began to dissolve. As his fingers dropped to the buttons on her nightshirt, she trembled and wondered crazily what he was likely to say when he came to her bedsocks. Her feet squirmed together, endeavouring to push the offending articles off before he ran across them, until it occurred to her that her pedestrian apparel was the very least of what she had to worry about. Suppose she froze up on him? Suppose he realised just how very inexperienced she was? Dear God, how could he not realise?

'You're shaking like a leaf.' His deep-pitched drawl was disarmingly gentle.

'I'm cold,' she lied.

Hovering on the edge of flight, she collided involuntarily with dark magnetic eyes that compelled and controlled. Her heartbeat hung in suspension. He touched a teasing fingertip to her taut lower lip. 'Would you like me to take your socks off for you?'

'Jake...I...oh...' Without making any effort to match the offer to action, he had lowered his head to let his lips hotly explore the slim arc of her throat. Her skin had acquired an unbearable sensitivity. She melted from outside in, completely losing the thread of what she had intended to say.

He eased apart the edges of her shirt to expose the swelling fullness of her breasts. Black hair brushed her chin as he ran his tongue oh, so lightly down the valley between the ripe mounds of creamy flesh. His thumbs grazed over her taut nipples and her hands dug into his shoulders in an unconscious revelation of frenzied need. His mouth fastened to a pink swollen peak and a torment of sweet sensation rippled drugging waves through her quivering limbs. For an instant she thought she might die of the pleasure he was giving her.

Her fingers knotted into his hair and she arched up to find the heated oblivion of his mouth again for herself. Her every skin cell was impatient, greedy, and that first scorching contact with his hard, masculine body excited her beyond bearing. Her hand ran down the length of his spine to press him still closer. Her abandonment jerked a stifled groan from him. The intimate proof of his desire for her was pushing against her stomach, sending her temperature shooting higher. The hand following the curve of her hip to the damp meeting of her thighs stilled as he dragged his mouth free of hers. 'Slow down,' he breathed raggedly. 'I want this to be perfect.'

Imperfect for Kitty was an inch of separation from any part of him. Her passion-glazed eyes focused on him.

'Don't stop,' she framed tightly, and reaching up she mated her tongue deeply with his to extract a soul-deep moan of response from him.

The skill of his exploring fingers drove out the last remnants of her control. What she was feeling could not be contained. A wild, tortured hunger guided her restive, pleading movements, inciting him to the same impatience. He found the rounded softness of her hips and pulled her to him. Kneeling between her thighs, he entered her, and suddenly he was there where she most needed him to be in a piercing, awesome surge of masculine power.

A split second of unexpected discomfort dredged a strangled gasp from her, but the thrusting urgency of his possession submerged the pang in a heady, exultant flood of almost agonising pleasure. She hadn't believed that there could be anything more, and then all of a sudden she was flying into the burning heat of the sun to shatter into a million glittering pieces in a climax so intense that she was utterly overwhelmed.

She floated back to the real world again. He was heavy in the tight circle of her arms, his face buried in her hair, the smooth skin of his back damp with perspiration beneath her spread fingers. An urge to smother him with grateful kisses and verbally bombard him with her love threatened her instantaneously. Her teeth connected painfully with her wayward tongue. If she had considered herself weak before this hour, she understood now that she was infinitely weaker in its aftermath. The powerful emotions flooding her demanded expression, not denial.

Releasing her of his weight, he stared searchingly down at her. His eyes veiled, a muscle pulling at the corner of his mouth as he breathed, 'You were nervous because it was a disaster the last time.'

'Was it?' Dialogue was beyond her. She didn't want to think; she didn't want to talk. She just wanted him to hold her.

'My ego's not that tender. If my memory serves me correctly, I hurt you a lot. I was drunk and I didn't have much experience.' The suggestion of honesty via gritted teeth larded his intonation. 'I was half crazy with wanting you and I lost my head——'

'Do we have to talk about this?' she interrupted.

He was cruel enough to push her hair off her cheek and deprive her of all natural concealment. His eyes were darkened pools of thoroughly determined gold. It seemed to her that, while she had shrunk in stature by placing herself in an indefensible position, Jake had gathered strength from the ease of his conquest. The idea left a nasty taste in her mouth.

'You don't need to talk. You only need to listen.'

She turned away from him, savaged by the lowering acknowledgement that once again she had given herself too lightly. 'I don't want to listen either!'

A ruthless hand connected with her shoulder and unceremoniously pushed her flat against the pillows again. 'Tough,' he said succinctly. 'You're not wearing the trousers in this relationship. Lie there and listen. I've lived with that night on my conscience for a very long time. I hated myself for it. You were sweet and innocent and no way were you ready for a physical relationship, but if there's a red-blooded male within a thousand miles of here who could have withstood the encouragement you gave me that night, I'd like to meet him!'

Her absolute silence inflamed him. His mouth tightened. 'I'm only asking you to put that night in some kind of perspective. When you ran away from home, I was worried half out of my mind about you. I blamed myself and I still blame myself. No comment?' he almost snarled down at her. 'Damn you, why are you freezing me out again?'

When he had supposedly been worrying himself out of his mind he had still been in the honeymoon phase with Liz. Scorn and pain mingled in her retort. 'Just because we've slept together, it doesn't mean you're entitled to——'

'Talk?' he cut in derisively. 'Or stake a claim on you? Is that what's really worrying you? That there might be strings attached?'

Scalding moisture lashed her partly lowered eyelids. Two minutes of conversation and they were circling each other like wolves again, ready to claw to the death for supremacy. Only this time she knew that defeat would be hers. She was in no state to match his rhetoric. 'I don't want to talk about the past. How many times do I have to tell you that?'

'Do you count Maxwell a part of that past? Or are you hoping that he's still hovering on the horizon?' he demanded roughly.

She wrenched the rumpled sheet back and rolled off the bed in one driven motion. 'You don't own me. You don't have any rights over me. Grant is none of your business!'

Snatching up her shirt, she fled downstairs. Shakily she pulled on the garment in front of the low-burning kitchen fire. Painful emotions were gusting through her in debilitating waves. He would leave. He had got what he wanted and more. She shuddered. To think of the gift of her body in such terms was degrading, but she was lacerated by the awareness that she had betrayed every atom of her desperate uncontrollable hunger for him.

Wouldn't he just love to learn in addition that Grant was her father? That Heaven might play the sultry man-killer on screen, but that Kitty at the age of twenty-five had less experience of men than many a teenager? Her blossoming sexuality had been cruelly arrested at seventeen. And out of fear she had kept herself inviolate from further masculine threat, only to surrender all over again to the same renegade male. What did that say about her moral fibre?

He might as well have put a cattle brand on her hip all those years ago, she reflected in sick despair. She belonged to him still. Heart and soul and body. She was as obsessed by Jake now as she had been in her teens, and once again Jake was the dominant partner—an inequality that shrivelled her pride and her confidence.

'By my code that bed we just shared makes Maxwell my business,' a cool, hard voice drawled.

She leapt up off her knees, clumsily holding her unbuttoned shirt closed. His bare feet had been soundless on the stairs. He had pulled on his jeans. In the moonlight he was a half dark, half silver pagan outline less than a foot from her.

As she went to step back, powerful hands clamped to her waist. Indifferent to her gasp of alarm, he lifted her and plonked her down on the edge of the table behind her. His leashed anger beat down at her from his fierce stare. 'Now you may find that attitude out of date,' he continued with galling evenness. 'But that's the way I feel and I'm not likely to change either. Have you been in contact with Maxwell?'

'Let me down!' she spluttered furiously.

'I want an answer first,' he said grimly.

'No!'

'No, you're not giving me an answer? Or no, you haven't been in touch with him?' he prompted.

'No, I haven't been in touch with him.' It was a driven surrender, enforced by the humiliating position he had her in.

He freed the small hands he had pinned flat to the table surface and her palms instantly flew up to lodge against his chest, seeking to push him away. 'That's all I wanted to know. You were the one to make a drama out of it,' he murmured infuriatingly as he eased his hands under her thighs, tugging her forward into the cradle of his pelvis.

'What are you doing, for God's sake?' she gasped.

He bent his dark head to do something sinfully erotic to her earlobe. Laughter shook him as an agonised ache of anticipation uncurled in her belly. Feverishly disorientated by his swing from threat to passion, she uttered a stifled negative which he completely ignored. The force of his mouth thrust her head back. He devoured her with the hot, rapacious intimacy of a lover and she went boneless, her defensive fingers unbracing to slide weakly down to his flat stomach, feeling his muscles jerk in reaction to the accidental caress.

'God, I want you all over again,' he groaned, bending her back over his supportive arm to send his lips travelling over her bared breasts, his tongue lashing wetly over her urgently sensitive nipples. Crying out, she clutched at his thick hair.

He wrapped her legs round his lean hips and carried her upstairs that way while he told her with a lack of inhibition that both shocked and excited her exactly what he planned to do next. Her aroused body had the consistency of melted honey heated to boiling-point when he tumbled her down on the bed. She sought him blindly with her hands but he would not be hurried. His control was infinitely stronger than hers.

Storm after storm of drowning sensation had alternately ravished and inflamed her before her sobbed pleas brought an end to the torture. He plunged into her and her nails scored his back. A sound between anguish and ecstasy escaped her. Her every sense was abandoned and

attuned to the raw physical reality of his body moving
on and within hers, hard and fast and then soft and slow
until she bit his shoulder in a torment of frustration and
the game stopped as he drove deep into her silken sheath.
What she had dimly believed couldn't happen again
happened in an agony of intense fulfilment as con-
vulsive pleasure shuddered through her.

Dawn had fought the darkness for a long time while
she lay, content just to look at him. His arm was a heavy
anchor across her, his dark, tousled head resting against
her shoulder. He slept in an extravagant sprawl, taking
up most of the bed. Her fingertips itched to trace the
straight, uncompromising jut of his nose and the
stubborn angle of his stubbled jawline.

Sleep had been impossible for her. There was a sense
of almost childish wonder that he was actually there in
the flesh beside her. Eight years of feverishly suppressed
need and longing were running riot with her emotions.
To lose a single precious moment in sleep would have
been heresy. She was extremely uncomfortable, pinned
to the lumpy edge of the mattress, but she could have
lain still on bare boards with alacrity because he was
holding her close. Oh, yes, this was love, great rolling
breakers of feeling flooding her with a strength that only
increased by the hour.

Was it really like last night for everybody? she wondered still in a partial daze. An insatiable passion, never
entirely damped down, never completely satisfied? He
had reached for her again and again. How many women
had experienced that same mindless satisfaction in Jake's
arms? Stiffening, she struggled to bury that first unwelcome shard of disquiet and insecurity, but it was
swiftly followed by another.

Paula appreciates her freedom as much as I do, he
had told her bluntly yesterday. Oh, why did she have to
remember that now? Why did she have to remember that

tomorrow and the next day weren't ringed on Jake's calendar with her name beside them? Hot-blooded sensuality lay at the very core of Jake's temperament. He was a very physical male with a strong sexual appetite. Why was she lying here like a lovesick, dreaming idiot with her heart in her eyes?

Jake had simply taken what he considered to be on offer. He hadn't intended to become involved with her. At the start he had avoided her. But somewhere along the line he had decided that she was a permitted weakness. For one night? Two nights? She inched dully out of the seductive warmth of his hold. Her glow of unreasoning euphoria had ebbed through the intrusive bars of reality. Jake didn't love her. He wanted her. Nothing had changed.

Last night she had faithfully promised herself that she would still leave. A desperate promise made by a desperate lady, fearfully accepting that she had lost all control of her emotions. On tiptoe she crept into the bathroom with an armful of clothes. Daylight shed a humiliating clarity on their respective motivations. Jake drew her like a magnet to her own downfall. When this ended the grief would be hers, not his, and she couldn't blame him for it this time. The scenario was all of her own making. She should never have come back.

She hunched knee to chin in a shallow bath, angry with herself, hating herself, but the effect of both sensations effectively cancelled out by the tormenting awareness of how much she loved him. As she was climbing out of the bath, water sloshing noisily about in spite of her efforts to be quiet, her ears pricked up at what she briefly thought was the phone ringing. She listened to silence and then towelled herself dry, certain she had been mistaken. Dressed, she padded out on to the landing like a sneak-thief. She didn't really want him to wake up. Awake he had to be faced.

The bedroom door was ajar, no longer closed as she had left it. With his back to the doorway, Jake was zipping up his jeans although he must have heard her entry.

'You're leaving?' Nothing like stating the obvious, Kitty, she thought with an inner groan. 'Don't you want...breakfast?' she enquired awkwardly.

Silence...seething silence. Rock-hard tension had brought the muscles into prominence on the long, virile sweep of his back. Distractedly noticing the little parallel scratchmarks she had left on his smooth skin, she reddened.

He swung round to snatch up his shirt. 'You lied to me!' he bit out in savage condemnation.

Astonished by the attack, she blinked bemusedly. 'Lied?'

'When did you phone Maxwell to tell him where you were?' His clenched features were a mask of dark fury.

Her brain was working in slow motion. 'But I didn't...the phone!' Eyes wide with horror, she grasped that she had indeed heard the phone earlier. 'Grant? Grant phoned? And you answered...oh, God,' she muttered in cringing conclusion.

His white teeth were a feral slash against his dark skin. 'You went crawling back to him, didn't you?'

Her palms pressed to her hot face. 'What did he say?'

'Well, let's put it this way, he didn't sound his usual oily, self-satisfied self when I cut the connection,' he imparted with derision. 'In fact he displayed an amazing amount of shock and disbelief for a creep who's been cheating on you from day one!'

She was feeling sick. 'What did you say to him?'

A black brow ascended. 'He wanted to know what I was doing here at this hour and I told him. He was still raging when I put the phone down,' he murmured scornfully. 'I doubt if he'll be very forgiving. He's ninety-nine per cent ego.'

Numbly she shook her head.

'I swear I don't know how he found out where I was!' she burst out. 'He must have guessed. It was probably him who tried to phone me last night but I didn't get there in time to answer it.'

Jake loosed his pent-up breath in an aggressive hiss. 'What a shame. A case of bad timing if ever I heard it!'

'I didn't have to tell you the truth!' she said painfully.

He searched her eyes fiercely. 'If I thought for one moment that you were lying to me...' He left the threat hanging and visibly ground his teeth together. 'If I've misjudged you, I ought to apologise.'

She waited.

'How the hell do you think I felt answering the phone to that bastard?' he vented instead, and strode past her into the bathroom.

What must her father be thinking? Had he realised it was Jake? There was only one parallel between Jake and Grant—a mutual loathing for the merest mention of the other's name. She sighed. She should have phoned Grant long before now. He didn't hold spite. She had never really believed for a second that he would cut her completely out of his life. But he had hurt her, and when Kitty was hurt it took her a long time to emerge from her defensive shell again.

When Jake came downstairs, she was replenishing the fire. Covertly she glanced at him, absorbing the brooding stillness of his stance. He had an explosive temper. A volcanic brilliance still lingered in his dark scrutiny even though he had backed down. 'I'm sorry I shouted at you, but his was the last voice on this earth that I wanted to hear.'

Razor-taut, she murmured, 'Would you like some coffee?'

'You don't want to know what I feel.' His handsome mouth twisted sardonically. 'That would be breaching the limits you've set us. Narrow, nasty little limits they are too. Believe it or not, I didn't come here last night solely to make love to you.'

Somehow he was putting her in the wrong and she resented that. Strung up with nervous tension, she said, 'No?'

'No! I don't want an affair with you,' he countered harshly.

Dumbly she looked at him all at sea. 'Do you want coffee?' she asked again, desperate to fill up the silence and not even appreciating how ridiculous the question sounded.

He swore under his breath and fixed her with a bitingly aggressive stare. 'I want to marry you.'

Her mouth opened and shut again soundlessly. For a stricken second she suspected him of cracking a macabre black joke at her expense.

'And if you laugh, so help me God, Kitty, you'd better do it from behind a steel-plated door this time,' he warned.

It was the most extraordinary proposal of marriage she had ever heard—the only one. She couldn't have laughed to save her life. He had shocked her witless. He stood tall, rock-steady and straight. The vulnerability in his unshielded gaze was hard, not soft. He expected her to turn him down. It wouldn't break him. Jake was a survivor. Tarrant pride and Tarrant obstinacy were an unbeatable combination.

Her tongue wet her lips in a snaking forage. She was feeling faint, a rushing noise interfering with her hearing. 'Are you saying that you're in love with me?'

He stared steadily back at her. 'I'm saying no to some grubby little affair with no commitment on either side. I want an end to sleepless nights and futile arguments.

I'd like you to be there when I wake up in the morning. I want to make a life with you,' he stated levelly. 'I don't care if you're on the rebound from Maxwell. I still think we've got enough to build on.'

Her restless fingers rubbed abstractedly at an old scorch mark on the scarred table. 'After one night?'

'I've never wanted a woman as much as I want you. I can admit that. You've haunted me for eight years and, after last night, you'll probably haunt me for the next eighty, but there's a lot more to marriage than sex.' Ebony-framed dark eyes intercepted her under-the-lashes glance and held it by pure force of will. 'I would still want to buy this place from you. I wasn't thinking of it as your dowry.'

Hot pink banished her pallor. 'Jake, that's not——'

He forged on in a gritty drawl. 'And by the way, Liz's inheritance is all tied up in a trust fund for Tina. I put it there. I never touched a penny of it while Liz was alive and I didn't change my mind when she was gone.'

Dear heaven, he still had small grasp of her real financial situation. She was a wealthy woman, some might say a very wealthy woman. Would he have proposed if he had known her true worth? Would she be more desirable or less desirable to him? A sick nausea cramped her stomach. Had he learnt his lesson with Liz? And had not her own past taught her an even harder lesson? Jake had not wanted her baby and then he had not even considered asking her to be his wife.

'You don't love me.' In her turmoil she barely knew what she was saying. It was difficult enough to actually accept that they were having this conversation.

He vented a humourless laugh. 'Are you telling me that I'd win points with you if I said I did?'

'No. I'm grateful that you didn't mention anything like that,' she whispered truthfully.

'Meaning?' he queried curtly.

'You were with Paula only a few days ago,' she protested, tautly defensive.

'Paula's a red herring,' he dismissed abrasively. 'I didn't come to your bed fresh from another woman's.'

'No,' she conceded half under her breath.

'You wanted me, Kitty. Just as much as I wanted you.'

Colouring, she walked over to the window. He had thrown the unanswerable and he knew it. 'That still doesn't mean that I'd want to marry you.'

'But it does mean more than you're prepared to admit. Why me?' he asked silkily. 'I don't believe you've had a whole host of lovers anywhere except in your own imagination.'

'I've been in a very emotional state of mind recently.' She stumbled over the confession in her haste to deflect him from that dangerous line of enquiry.

Firm hands spun her back to face him. She pulled away, drifting hurriedly out of reach. If he touched her, it would be fatal. Before she knew where she was, she would be feeding the hens for Jessie and sewing on his buttons. Her efforts to inwardly arouse her own sense of humour fell on stony ground. Her thoughts were too centred on panic and another emotion that she flatly refused to recognise.

His attention did not stray from her flushed profile. 'There's also Tina to consider. And your career. I'd be surprised if you couldn't get television work here in the UK...'

Kitty would have been astonished. *The Rothmans* had turned her into a household name. Jake was really talking about something which he knew precious little about.

'But I'll be frank. I don't fancy a commuter marriage. At least not in the beginning. It wouldn't be giving us much of a chance. It's something we'd have to discuss,' he completed unemotionally.

She turned away again, wishing that he would stop watching her. All he lacked was an interrogator's light, and she was desperate to hide the tumultuous state of her emotions. But no ... no, she wasn't even toying with the idea of saying yes. She wasn't that stupid. Absolutely not, absolutely not that stupid by any stretch of the imagination. She cleared her throat, steadied by the inner certainty. 'I don't really see myself as housewife material.'

'There is such a thing as compromise. I can manage to maintain a housekeeper and a wife,' he said drily. 'Just as you could manage to have a career without putting in a seven-day week.'

'An acting career requires one hundred per cent commitment. If you can't be in the right place at the right time as often as the opportunity comes up, you might as well forget about it,' she countered, and as swiftly questioned why she was bothering to argue.

He expelled his breath. 'I thought you wanted to be a writer.'

'I mightn't make it as a writer.' She ran her fingers jerkily through her hair. 'I don't know why I'm even talking about this.'

She was moving about the room in an aimless circle, giving his tall, dark figure as wide a berth as possible. He had the element of surprise when he caught her to him with a lean hand and probed her mouth in a shockingly hungry assault. Her resistance was nil. Her fingers slid beneath his jacket and burrowed helplessly under his shirt to find skin. Crushed to the all-male heat of his long, powerful length, she was in seventh heaven. Her sensory perceptions centred entirely on him within seconds. The room, the hour and the reasons why she had been trying to avoid this exact development vanished along with self-dominion.

* * *

She awoke from an uneasy slumber alone. As she sat up, she reeled dizzily and lifted a questing hand to her woozy head. She wasn't feeling very well. Understatement. She was feeling ghastly. Shivering, she crawled out of bed to plug in the electric fire. Every aching muscle she possessed complained at the activity. A hot drink. That was what she needed.

Dear God, how long had she slept? It was late afternoon and she had only the vaguest recollection of Jake's departure. Weak and perspiring from the virulent cold symptoms assailing her, she went downstairs.

The phone was making a peculiar noise. The receiver was hooked off the cradle. Jake must have left it that way. With a rueful hand she replaced it. While she was still in mental turmoil Jake had ruthlessly swept her back to bed. Within twenty-four hours he had separated her from sanity. In the night desire had a silent voice sufficient to quiet her misgivings... but at four in the afternoon she was appalled by the extent of the power he had over her. He had mentioned marriage and what common sense she had retained had gaily gone walkabout.

That final, treacherous surrender of hers could conceivably have convinced him that she was thinking in terms of a positive answer. In actuality, if she was brutally honest with herself, she hadn't had to think at all. Within her heart her answer had never been in doubt, but she had an instinctive terror of such inner promptings.

His proposal could only have been motivated by the devastating physical hunger they shared. In other words, demeaning as the thought was, Jake was currently a slave to his own sexual appetite. After a failed marriage of convenience with Liz, he doubtless didn't think that he could have very much to lose in a second risky venture.

In addition he was violently jealous of Grant. How much had her father's phone call contributed to Jake's primitively possessive need to mark her out as exclusively his property? Hadn't this morning merely been an agonising replay of an eight-year-old catastrophe? A drunk had tried to kiss her and Jake had gone overboard, crossing the boundary lines he had carefully set up between them over the preceding months.

She flinched as the phone trilled an intrusive summons. It was cowardice, but she didn't want to answer it. The persistent trill needled her sore head. With an exclamation of defeat she lifted the receiver.

'Miss Colgan?' Grant's stalwart secretary, Becky, sounded unusually harassed and waited for Kitty to confirm her presence before saying with ritualistic precision, 'Call from Mr Maxwell.'

'Don't even think of telling me that I'm not entitled to demand an explanation!' Grant's transatlantic drawl sizzled down the line with whiplash accuracy and pitch. 'Tarrant!' A harsh expletive seared her sensitive eardrums.

She put a hand up to her throbbing brow. It came away wet with perspiration. It was little wonder that her brain had the elasticity of sludge, she thought dully. 'He's not married any more,' she said tightly.

'Is that supposed to make me feel better? Have you gone right out of your mind?' he demanded. 'I tried to stop you going back up there. Why didn't you listen to me?'

She decided that he might as well have the lot at once. 'I still love him.'

'Oh, my God.' It was an agonised groan and she could picture his handsome face, composed in pained lines of cynicism and scorn, discomfiture lurking somewhere at the back of his green eyes. With the sole exception of anger, overt emotion made Grant extremely ill at ease.

'That's how I feel,' she persisted unsteadily. 'I won't let you put me down.'

'By the sound of it, you don't need my assistance to do that,' he parried with cutting satire. 'We may have had our disagreements recently, but I've never been less than straight with you.'

'I don't need this right now,' she muttered wearily. 'I just wanted to be honest with you.'

'Honesty like that I can do without. You're making a complete ass of yourself. I suppose you do realise that?' he probed with remorseless contempt. 'Do you need your memory refreshed? He ran rings round you and he dumped you, Kitty. He probably hasn't that in mind this time. After all, you've had your rough edges smoothed off and you just happen to be worth a few million. I'm not surprised to hear that he's made a move on you, but I'm very surprised that you can be feeble enough to fall for the same lines a second time.'

Static buzzed on the line. In an expression of silent torment, she had squeezed her eyes shut. Not one derisive word had missed target. 'Stop it,' she whispered.

'I'm sorry if you don't like the bad news, but I'm damned if I'm going to apologise for it,' he continued hardly. 'What is it about this guy? You could have any man you wanted and yet it's still him. Is he the one that got away? If this is an ego trip I could understand that, but I don't understand anything else.'

'You never have understood me,' she murmured tautly.

'You've been working too hard, Kitty. I'll even allow that maybe I put on too much pressure there for a time,' he conceded, obviously feeling generous after shredding her. 'Pull yourself together and jump on the first plane over here, hmm? It's too late for the film but I wouldn't say no to a house guest. Your agent's been in touch with me. There's an offer of a mini-series pending...'

'I can't leave, I can't run away from this!'

'Tell him to drop dead and then catch the plane,' Grant suggested drily. 'I'm really not particular about how you do it. How's the great literary work going?'

She started to tell him, but he wasn't interested enough to listen and he cut her off to talk about his film. Ten minutes later, she slumped down in sick dizziness on the settee. She had never felt more alone and isolated. Or more wretched. Feeble, yes, she supposed, looking back over the past weeks; feeble was almost too kind a description.

There had never been the remotest possibility of her marrying Jake. Not a spoken-out-loud possibility. Did she punish herself now for harbouring a dream? A loveless union with Jake would kill her by degrees. Inch by inch, hour by hour. She attempted to console herself with the knowledge of the misery she would save herself from by cutting loose now. But since the prospect of not seeing him again today, never mind tomorrow, was capable of depressing her, it was a rather pointless procedure.

He had mentioned something about a trip to York and he was sure to be working tonight. She would leave tomorrow first thing. She had to make herself believe that. Staggering upright, she lifted the first two chapters of her book off the dresser and thrust the folder beneath her portable typewriter. She trudged out to the car with her burden. Her legs threatened to crumple under her and she sagged back down on to the settee again to catch her breath.

In a minute she would go back upstairs and pack. By tomorrow she was sure to be feeling stronger. She wasn't planning to join her father in the South of France. But in her disorientation her lack of a decided destination really didn't seem at all important. The minute of rest slid unnoticed into a few minutes and her aching eyes slowly closed.

She awakened without ever knowing she had been asleep, and she couldn't breathe; she couldn't breathe at all. Her fingers torturously clawed at the fabric beneath her cheek in a weak attempt to raise herself. The rasping agony of her own lungs controlled her. Her frantic movements sent her rolling on to the floor, the invisible smoke in the darkness choking her.

Glass splinters flew out from the window. Hands dragged at her. She didn't feel them. The top of her head was flying off and she lapsed into unconsciousness.

CHAPTER EIGHT

SOMEBODY was shouting at Kitty, shaking her. She started to cough and gasp in wrenching, painful spasms that jerked her whole body. She recognised Jake's arms by sense and touch alone, her eyes opening on a blurred vision of the night that was reminiscent of a view of hell. It was no longer dark. Incredible noise was bombarding her ears. A fizzling and a crackling joined in the roar of the orange and yellow flames shooting up into the skies, sending multi-coloured sparks showering down in all directions. She couldn't see the cottage, couldn't even grasp that it was in there somewhere feeding the thick, swirling smoke and the awesome flames.

There was a sudden flash and an ear-splitting report and she ducked her head into the shelter of Jake's jacket, her arms tightening round him as she gasped for oxygen that hurt her raw throat. He was trembling against her and she could feel the ferocious anger he was fighting to contain. He was struggling to breathe and shout at the same time and somebody was bundling her into a blanket.

She wasn't sure whether that somebody was Jake or not. She was floating in a poppy field awash with glorious scarlet flowers, the sun a drenching warmth on her skin. She couldn't see Jake, but she could sense his presence. It was a paradise of a place and the far-off voices around her penetrated her mystic vision not at all.

'Yes,' she croaked to nobody in particular. 'I said yes.'

She surfaced briefly in a strange, brightly lit room. Hazily she focused on Jake. His face was all black. He

132

was arguing about something. A female in a white coat as wide as she was tall was towering over his chair, loudly telling him not to be obstreperous. She couldn't keep her eyes open on that intriguing sight. With a little smile she drifted off again in search of her poppy field.

'How does you feel?'

An anxious little face was hovering over her. Tina? With a groan, Kitty moved her head. Her temples pounded and there was a razor at the back of her throat. She winced.

'Are you really coming to live at my house forever and ever?' Tina demanded excitedly.

'Put it like that and she might change her mind.' Jake appeared and swept Tina off the bed. He gave her a hug before setting her down again. 'Go and ask Jessie very nicely for a cup of tea.'

Kitty plucked at the duvet and stole a dazed look round the pleasantly furnished unfamiliarity of her surroundings. 'Where am I?' she whispered.

'Torbeck. It's five in the afternoon, day one after the conflagration.'

Her brow indented. She had only the haziest memory of it all, disconnected snatches that didn't make much sense. 'You mean,' she swallowed with difficulty, 'it was real—there really was a fire?'

'Either that or there are an awful lot of people suffering from a mass hallucination.' Poised at the foot of the bed, he surveyed her, his dark beautiful eyes intent on her pallor. 'I've spent most of the day dealing with the police and the fire department. I'm afraid they arrived too late. The house is a shell. Everything's gone,' he told her almost conversationally. 'Do you realise just how lucky you are to be alive?'

She pushed a shaking hand through her tangled hair. 'My God...the last thing I recall is sitting on the

settee...well, there are one or two other bits...' her voice
tailed off.

'You have Tina's flu. Of course it would never have
occurred to you to call a doctor,' he breathed, flexing
long fingers expressively on the brass foot-rail of the bed.
'The fire started in your bedroom. You wouldn't have
had a prayer if you'd been up there.'

Her evasive gaze arrowed to the sprigged floral pattern
on the duvet. 'I left the electric fire burning,' she
mumbled.

'Correction,' he contradicted. 'You left a faulty electric
fire burning. Your grandmother put it away. She knew
it was dangerous but she was too stingy to dump anything!' A rise of strong emotion was betrayed by the
ground-out syllables. 'If the door between the hall and
the kitchen hadn't been shut, you'd be dead.'

Her stomach was feeling fragile. 'Will you stop saying
that?'

'I just want it to sink in. I got you out with minutes
to spare,' he advanced tautly.

'I wasn't feeling well. I forgot that I'd put on the fire
to heat the room.'

'You got a good, roasting blaze going, I'll give you
that!' he grated in a driven undertone. 'I warned you
about the wiring—it must be fifty years old.'

'You got me out,' she grasped, eager to take him off
the subject. 'You risked your own——'

His eyes were fierce. 'There was nothing heroic about
it. I don't remember getting out of the car. I don't remember kicking in the window. The only thing I remember is thinking that I'd pulled out a dead body.'

A shudder slivered through her. 'You shouted at me.'

'It may surprise you, but the prospect of life without
you didn't enthrall me,' he bit out jerkily. 'And the
shouting came later, after you had revived. I didn't realise
you were sick until you folded on me.'

'I'm sorry,' she said tightly.

Silence dragged. He sighed. 'I'm not. I've got you under my roof.'

He settled down on the edge of the bed and pulled her confidently into his arms. With a shaky little sigh she subsided against him, having no objections to reassurance when it was forced on her. She rested her chin on a broad shoulder sheathed in fine wool. A feathery strand of black hair brushed her cheek. The familiar scent of his body, deliciously clean, gloriously familiar, enclosed her. She had a stark recollection of him shaking against her last night and her lips wanted to turn inwards to his cheek.

If she hadn't been downstairs, he would have tried to go upstairs to find her. She knew that as instinctively as she knew that the sun would rise every morning. He wouldn't have counted the possible cost to himself. For perhaps the first time she attempted to equate the fact that he would risk his life for her with that terrible rejection he had dealt her in the past. And it was like trying to bring two sides of a triangle together. Or match two radically different personalities. She wondered in frustration if there really could be some less obvious explanation for the way he had treated her, something he might have told her if she hadn't stopped him in his tracks.

She parted her dry lips on a very leading question. 'Is having me under your roof...important to you?'

He was so quiet, so very quiet, she stiffened. 'It's an absolute necessity for a husband and wife,' he drawled just above her head.

She had a crazed mental image of her ears shooting out on stalks. 'A husband and wife?' she parroted.

'You said you'd marry me.'

'Did I?' she muttered in a stupor.

'Yes. You did. I knew you would.' As he made the confirmation he held her back from him. Black lashes

were narrowed over piercing dark eyes. 'And you're
going through with it. I didn't spend all of yesterday
making wedding arrangements just so that you could
decide to change your mind last minute.'

'Wedding arrangements?' she gulped. 'Yesterday?'

The faintest colour highlighted his angular cheekbones. 'I didn't see any reason to hang around. You
ought to be lying down.' He settled her back against the
pillows as if she were a rag doll and tucked the duvet
round her slight frame. 'What was your typewriter doing
in your car?' he shot at her abruptly.

'How would I know? I don't know what I was doing
last night . . . yesterday!' For some reason tears flooded
her eyes and rolled down her cheeks in embarrassing riv-
ulets as she turned her head away in desperation from
him. 'I wasn't feeling well; I wasn't myself.'

'You were probably more yourself than you've been
in a long time. You kept on smiling at me. Who am I
to complain if it takes a temperature of a hundred and
two to do it?' Long fingers smoothly massaged the
knotted tension from her spine. He told her that she was
suffering from shock, that tears were quite normal, but
she wasn't listening. The fire preoccupied her jumbled
thoughts less than the bombshell he had calmly dropped
on her unprepared head.

Had she said she would marry him? Somewhere in
that poppy field where there was no shadow of the past,
no Grant to bulldoze her dreams back into the dust?
Without Jake tomorrow and the next day and the day
after that would be empty. She faced an inescapable truth
that deprived her of choice and made decision super-
fluous. The prospect of those empty tomorrows
stretching endlessly before her was too terrifying to
contemplate.

'Dr Cates, the family GP, checked you over last night.
I assumed that you wouldn't want to go to hospital unless

it was strictly necessary. The Press would've been on to the story immediately,' he pointed out.

She sighed. 'News of the fire is bound to escape.'

He strolled over to the low, deep-silled window. 'That's possible, but there's no real story to be had. Merrill's husband, John, arrived at Lower Ridge before the police. At my request he drove your car over here, and the car was the only proof that you were, in fact, in the house at the time of the fire. You haven't been bothered by the authorities because, as far as they're concerned, you'd already gone off somewhere for a few days.'

His speedy response to the threat of media interest in the chaos of the previous night astonished her. 'They think I went off and left a fire burning?'

An expressive brow arched. 'Stranger things have happened. In any case, the police lost interest once they were satisfied that there was nothing suspicious about the fire. But for the cover-up this house would be besieged by reporters, clamouring for an interview with you after your ordeal.' He sent her a grim smile. 'You might have enjoyed the attention, but I wouldn't have. I don't intend to get married on Wednesday with a pack of reporters on the church steps.'

Her lashes swept up on startled violet eyes. 'Wednesday?' she cried. 'That's only three days away!'

Her disbelief had no visible impression on him. He looked steadily back at her. 'You have something better to do on Wednesday?'

'Be serious,' she urged weakly, certain he was teasing her. 'When you said wedding arrangements, I never dreamt that you . . .'

'Meant so soon?' His sensual mouth twisted. 'My uncle is a bishop. I saw him yesterday and I explained the situation. He completely understood our need for a quiet, quick ceremony. We've been granted a special licence.'

'But Wednesday...' she repeated helplessly.

'At the village church at eleven. I don't see the problem.'

She was not impervious to the warning edge of his intonation or the poised stillness of his stance. 'I didn't expect it to be so soon,' she muttered.

'We have only ourselves to please...don't we? Unless you're still keen to keep your options open...'

She glanced up, not mistaking his meaning, and her cheeks stained with colour. She was entrapped by the dark, unyielding force of his challenging appraisal and held by it to become equally sensitised to the electric sexuality he possessed. Her skin heated afresh, her pulse raced and rationality evaporated at a similar speed. Her head was starting to spin. He was so businesslike about it all. His no-frills-attached proposal had had a similar daunting practicality, but there was nothing cool about the leashed hunger of his stare.

'I should be getting up now,' she muttered, pushing back the duvet and finding herself unexpectedly plunged into sick dizziness as she sat up.

'Doctor's orders. You're not fit to get up yet.' Jake settled her back again, rearranging the bedclothes impatiently. 'You're underweight and you haven't been looking after yourself very well. You're not going to bounce back as quickly as Tina did.'

It was too much effort to argue. Jessie bustled in with a tray and Kitty did her best to eat the omelette that had been prepared for her. Afterwards she must have slept because when she wakened, drenched in perspiration from a nightmare, it was dark.

'Are you all right?' A finger of light left a path from the ajar door, silhouetting Jake.

'I had a dream...' Incredibly relaxed by his presence, she rested back again.

'I know. You were shouting at the top of your voice.'
Amusement threaded his voice as he settled beside her.
'Do you want me to get you a drink?'

'No,' she mumbled sleepily, reaching out a hand to
find a lean thigh. 'I didn't know where you were.'

'You'll feel better in the morning.'

Drowsily she smiled and snuggled up against him. 'I
feel better now.'

He woke her up with a cup of tea. He was fully
dressed, his dark hair still damp from a shower. He
smoothed the pillow indented with the evidence that she
had not slept alone and grinned, looking suddenly very
young. 'Jessie is not a liberated woman.'

'But we didn't . . .'

He captured her parted lips with drowning sweetness,
driving out all coherent thought and straightened again.
'Merrill's coming over to see that you take it easy.'

'Oh.' She swallowed, fingering the elaborate lace
bodice of the nightdress she had not until now had the
presence of mind to examine. 'Is this hers?'

'It's Sophie's.'

Kitty stiffened. 'Have you told her?' she demanded
abruptly.

'Merrill?'

'Your mother,' she murmured.

His narrowed eyes glittered down at her troubled face.
'Why? Do you think I needed to ask for permission? I
made the announcement the day before yesterday when
I was in York,' he drawled with an ironic smile.

'She must have been . . . shocked.'

'If she was, she didn't say so.' A chilling aspect had
tautened his dark, compelling features. 'You don't need
to worry about Sophie. After all, she won't be living
here and that certainly won't be a sacrifice for her.'

'Are you trying to find a nice way to tell me that she
won't accept me at all?' she prompted tightly.

His jawline squared. 'What I'm telling you is that it's a matter of supreme indifference to me whether she does or does not.'

'But I don't want to cause trouble between you,' she persisted.

He walked back to the door. 'I have to go out. I'll see you later.'

He had ignored her uneasy comments. Kitty had no pleasant memories of Sophie Tarrant, but she had never doubted the strength of Sophie's attachment to her only son. Jake's sudden decision to remarry, not to mention his choice of bride, would naturally have shocked and concerned his mother. Plainly Mrs Tarrant's attitude to her hadn't changed. What had changed to a quite astonishing degree was Jake's attitude to his mother. He made no allowances for the older woman's feelings and that surprised Kitty. Yet should it surprise her?

The forceful, aggressive side of Jake's powerful personality had grown infinitely more dominant over the past years. Had Liz done that to him? Endowed him with that core of angry, dark bitterness that Kitty had sensed in him more than once? Made him coldly, even callously indifferent towards his mother's feelings? Or had Sophie done that for herself? Kitty reminded herself that there had been conflict between mother and son over Liz long before she had come on the scene.

She got out of bed, still feeling ridiculously weak and shaky. She found the bathroom across the landing and, although the effort exhausted her, she took a quick shower. She was combing her hair in the bedroom when a plump blonde entered, carrying a tray. 'Gosh, I thought you'd still be in bed!'

The almost schoolgirlish exclamation made Kitty laugh. 'Merrill?'

Brown eyes twinkled ruefully at her. 'Don't say it. I've put on some weight since we last met. People have walked past me in the street without recognising me,' she confided. 'I can't stick to diets.'

Her easy warmth was a pleasant surprise to Kitty. As a child, Jake's sister had slavishly copied her mother in treating Kitty as someone quite beneath her notice. 'You shouldn't be running after me,' she said gently as Merrill smoothed a self-conscious hand over her pregnant stomach.

'You're very pale,' Merrill remarked. 'How are you feeling?'

'Not quite normal yet,' Kitty confided ruefully and accepted the tray.

Merrill took a seat on the blanket chest by the wall. 'You should be better in time for the wedding,' she quipped.

Kitty glanced up uncertainly. 'How do you feel about that? You can be frank.'

Merrill grimaced. 'Lord, when we were children, I must have been even more hideous to you than I remember for you to ask that. Whatever makes Jake happy makes me happy.'

'But you must be surprised...'

Merrill grinned. 'No, I have to say that I'm not. That's probably because when we were younger I always expected you and Jake to end up together...' Faltering badly as she realised what she'd said, she flushed uncomfortably and groaned, 'How to put your foot in your mouth in one easy lesson. Let me put it another way. If you're prepared to marry my brother and live up here, you must really care about him. It's hardly what you've been used to. It's a funny old world, isn't it? You went out and found fame and fortune and the Tarrants fell on hard times.' She wrinkled her nose. 'There's probably a moral there somewhere.'

'It was bad luck.'

Merrill sighed. 'Not really. If Jake hadn't been so determined that the rest of us came out of it all with some cash, he could have kept the Grange. It would've been a struggle for him then, but the bank still had faith in him,' she disclosed. 'If you ask me, it was his bad luck that he had an overdeveloped sense of responsibility. At the time we certainly weren't grateful to him. We wanted the house *and* the lifestyle we'd always had and he knew that we couldn't have both.'

Made grossly uncomfortable by Merrill's frank confidences, Kitty said in desperation. 'Do you work?'

'Not now, but I did work for John's father as a secretary.' Suddenly she grinned. 'How can you be so calm? Aren't you frantic about what you're going to wear on Wednesday? Every stitch you own has gone up in smoke!'

Kitty smiled at the younger woman's drama. 'The majority of my clothes are still in London. If I phone the housekeeper, she'll have them sent up.'

'But that could take days!' Merrill dismissed.

'No, I'll ring her now. She'll send them immediately.' Kitty hesitated, unwilling to say that for the right price the carrier would be eager to provide instant service.

'But you'll have to wear something special on Wednesday,' Merrill pressed. 'Actually there's something suitable right here under this roof. Jane had our great-grandmother's gown professionally restored for her wedding two years ago. She had to starve herself into it. The waist is absolutely tiny but I think it would fit you.'

'A wedding dress?' Kitty queried. 'I don't think Jake's expecting...'

Merrill laughed. 'I wasn't supposed to tell you, but it was his idea. I'd completely forgotten that it was here. I'll look it out later.'

If there was a dress available, the suggestion was only practical. Kitty smiled to herself. She refused even to think about how their marriage would affect her father and her future mother-in-law. When she had to, she would face those problems, but not now. Nothing would be allowed to spoil the next few days, she promised herself.

Since there was a phone by the bed, she called Mrs Stuart and made her request for her clothes. No sooner had she put the phone down than she was impulsively planning a second call, subdued excitement brimming in her thoughtful gaze. Merrill brought her some magazines and Jessie came upstairs with a pair of fuchsia-pink trousers and a sweatshirt.

'Jane left these behind the last time she was here, but you're not to be even thinking of getting up before lunch,' Jessie told her bossily.

As soon as Kitty was alone again, she lifted the phone. Mr Barker, who ran Colwell Holdings, was initially quite disconcerted to receive a personal call from her. He asked anxiously how he might be of assistance. Kitty breathed in deep and proceeded to tell him. She wanted a surveyor to go over the Grange and list the renovations and repairs required to put the house in order.

'I must warn you that you're talking about a considerable amount of costly work, Miss Colgan,' he said carefully.

'I don't expect the entire cost to be carried by the estate. I'll contact my accountant. There'll be no shortage of funds,' she asserted, and then added, 'By the way, I'm keen for the work to be started as soon as possible.'

She dozed a little, wakening to feel shamefully idle. Tina bounced into her room just as she had finished getting dressed. 'Jessie's putting your lunch on a tray,' she announced. 'You're s'posed to be in bed.'

'Where have you been all morning?'

'Playgroup,' Tina said dolefully, sliding a hand into Kitty's on the stairs. 'Daddy said I had to go.'

'You're home now,' Kitty pointed out cheerfully.

Tina brightened and asked if she wanted to see her kitten. Jessie appeared from the kitchen, irate that Kitty had left her bed.

'Jessie, if I lie in that bed any longer, I'll take root there.'

The older woman frowned. 'You should still be resting.'

Jake walked in, dark hair tousled by the breeze, and Kitty had an almost irresistible urge to fling herself into his arms. Embarrassed by the force of that prompting, she gave him a truculent smile. 'I'm not going back to bed.'

'Fine.' A lazy smile formed his sensual mouth. 'I'm free for the rest of the day.'

Warmth surged through her. Tina chattered constantly through the meal and, under the dark onslaught of Jake's unremittingly steady scrutiny, Kitty dizzily cleared her plate without even realising what she was eating. Jessie insisted on bringing them coffee in the lounge. Kitty sat down on a comfortable chesterfield and looked around herself with interest. She couldn't help picturing the contents restored to the more gracious setting of the Grange.

Guilty pink marked her complexion. She was being a little premature. 'Did you sell all the surplus furniture when you came here?'

'Yes. Sophie wanted to store it but I persuaded her that an auction would be wiser. The proceeds endowed her with a decent private income, without which frankly she couldn't have managed,' he said quietly. 'The family portraits are in the loft. Liz talked me into keeping them, but there's no room for them here. Sentiment's rarely practical.'

Kitty hid a private smile, already pleasantly engaged in envisaging the transformation soon to take place at the Grange. Tina joined them with her kitten, whispering, 'It's all right to bring him in when Granny isn't here, but you won't tell her, will you?'

Down on the floor, Kitty shook her head and thought murderous thoughts about a woman capable of putting that amount of fearful anxiety into a four-year-old's eyes. 'It'll be our secret,' she promised.

Tina wasn't slow to take advantage of the attention she was receiving. She brought her favourite toys down to show them off and, late afternoon, Jake breathed, 'She makes a better chaperon than Jessie,' with wry amusement. 'We'll go out to dinner tomorrow night.'

By nine in the evening, Kitty was feeling exhausted again. Jake took in her bruised eyes and sighed, 'You'd better turn in.'

Upstairs they checked on Tina and Kitty screened a yawn. 'I do feel like an early night.'

'It would be very selfish of me to tell you what I feel like.' Jake curved her into tantalising contact with his lean, hard length and she trembled, seduced by the heat of him so close.

'Would it be?' she whispered, leaning invitingly against him, weak with the wanting he could so easily invoke.

As his body reacted involuntarily to her proximity, Jake uttered a muted imprecation and set her back from him with a grim smile. 'Yes. It would be. If I touch you now, I'm going to spend the entire night in your bed and you're not likely to get much sleep,' he said bluntly. 'In any case, we'll be married in another forty-eight hours and I intend to do it by the book this time.'

His withdrawal sharply disconcerted her. He could plunge her into the wanton hold of a hunger that she couldn't control, and a part of her resented and feared that power he had at his fingertips. It was not at hers. And Kitty was innately sensitive to any hint of rejection.

He read the hurt and bewilderment in her eyes a
clearly as if she had spoken out loud, and suddenly h
crushed her to him before she could turn away and /h
was taking her mouth hungrily and fiercely, restrain
abandoned for several endless minutes. She was so weal
after that passionate assault that she swayed slightly, and
he ran a caressing hand over her flushed cheekbone, un
tamed sensuality in his smiling scrutiny. 'I'll see you in
the morning.'

After breakfast next day, Merrill arrived. 'You're in
the way, big brother,' she announced. 'We've go
wedding finery to try on.'

The Edwardian gown that had belonged to Jake':
great-grandmother was far too long. Jessie and Merril
were undeterred. The dress was pinned up and Jessie
settled herself in the lounge with a sewing box. Jake':
sister stayed for lunch and, as she was leaving, told Kitty
that she would be returning to take Tina home with her
later that day. 'We'll keep her until the end of next week.'

'Daddy s'plained it all,' Tina said mournfully. 'You
can't be a mummy for another week.'

Kitty hugged her, 'We'll see,' she whispered, reluctan
to interfere with Jake's arrangements, but worried that
by the end of the week Tina would be feeling unwanted.

Her clothes arrived in the afternoon. When the de-
livery men from the special express service had carried
in the last case, the entire hall was awash with luggage.

'Do you ever dump anything?' Jake enquired gently.

She decided not to tell him that there was almost as
much again in Grant's other home in Los Angeles. As
the heap of extracted garments grew higher on the bed,
she murmured, 'It's just a matter of sorting out what's
useful.'

A sure-fingered hand intercepted a swathe of jersey
split to the thigh and slashed to the waist. 'I'd lock you
in the cellar before I let you loose in that.'

'I wore it to one of Grant's premières.'

'And he bought most of this stuff for you, didn't he?' His dark gaze gleamed ferociously over her and she rather liked the sensation.

She lowered her head to another case, 'Yes.'

'There must be jewellery as well.'

She swallowed. 'It's still in London.'

'And it stays there. All of it,' he delivered with hard emphasis. 'It's not coming up here.'

In astonishment her head jerked up. 'I'm not parting with my jewellery!'

He hunkered down on a level with her. 'I'll put it another way. It's either it or me,' he drawled softly. 'Take your choice.'

Before she could voice a furious retort, the phone rang and he sprang up to answer it. Her treacherous gaze followed him. It was one of those little betraying habits she tried very hard to control, but her heart had a homing device planted on him. With a few words she could banish his brooding antipathy towards Grant and yet she couldn't make herself speak those words.

Jake was not one hundred per cent sure of her. That gave her an edge, an edge she was convinced she needed to hang on to him. When she had to tell him about Grant, she would find some other way to keep him slightly off balance. My God, clever women had been manipulating men for centuries, she told herself, and if other women could do it, she could do it. If she openly ceded him her love, her loyalty and her absolute commitment now, how much would he value them? How much had he valued those gifts in the past?

Jake was such a very physical male. His present intense desire for her would not last forever. As a teenager he had only had to lift a finger to attract any girl he had wanted. There had been so many of them that Kitty had been naïvely cheered by the fact that not a single one of

them could hold him. She wasn't now. She hadn't held
his interest either. She shivered, suddenly cold. When a
man has rejected a woman once, wouldn't it be ever
easier for him to do it a second time?

Had it been like this with Liz? A swift, hot passion
roused by sexual chemistry that finally flickered out and
died? She had cushioned only her own pride in striving
to believe that he had married Liz for money. How could
she believe that? He had sold up the estate to provide
for his mother and sisters. Jake's hot-blooded sensual
nature was far more likely to have thrust him into Liz's
arms just as it had once thrust him into a narrow bed
in an attic room. Had he ever been in love with any
woman? And was it insane of her to hope that given
time she might just succeed in winning that love where
once she had failed?

He came down beside her again, his dark, handsome
features ruefully cast. 'That was Barney.' He referred to
the third partner in the veterinary practice, whom she
had still to meet. 'I'm afraid I'll be covering for him
tonight.'

'Tonight?' she echoed in dismay. 'But we were going
out!'

Jake sighed. 'His father's had a massive heart attack
and he's not expected to live. I'm afraid our dinner date
will have to be shelved.' He paused before reluctantly
continuing, 'In fact, I doubt that I'll have any of the
time off that I had arranged over the next week.'

'You are kidding me,' Kitty breathed incredulously.

'We're very busy at this time of the year. Drew can't
cope on his own and I do have to pull my weight here
as well,' he reminded her wryly. 'I'll be taking over the
milking tomorrow so that John can have a lie-in for a
change.'

For the first time the hard realities of Jake's working
responsibilities impinged on her cosy little cocoon. He

was bent on tugging her into his arms. Playing for time, she settled a palm to his broad chest. 'I've been thinking about something...'

Displacing her hand with single-minded intent, he would have taken her mouth had she not turned her face aside. 'Obviously not what I've been thinking about.'

She plucked with taut fingers at one of his shirt buttons. 'It would be ridiculous for you to buy Lower Ridge from me. You should put that money into hiring someone to work with John. You're a vet, not a farmer.'

'Tell me,' he said shortly. 'Are you planning to sell your jewellery and endow me with that as well? I mean, it wouldn't be much use to you up here, would it?'

His hand had a painfully tight grip on her shoulder and she couldn't understand what was the matter with him. 'Now that you mention it...no, but——'

'But nothing,' he interrupted. 'Let's get one fact of life straight now. I keep you. You don't keep me.'

Her violet eyes sparkled. 'Another one of your old-fashioned principles?'

'Got it in one.' With a smouldering look, he released her and sprang up.

'I just made a very sensible suggestion,' she snapped, rising to her own feet. 'Marriage is all about sharing.'

'You can put the money in the bank. I won't be touching it.'

Inflamed, she said, 'And what if I've already got a lot of money in the bank?'

'That's an illogical question,' he bit out impatiently. 'You haven't, and if you had I wouldn't have asked you to marry me.'

'Oh, wouldn't you have?' she snapped in utter disbelief.

CHAPTER NINE

'No, I wouldn't have,' Jake repeated harshly. 'And when I do buy Lower Ridge, the money should go to Maxwell. He bought it for you.'

'Good God!' Kitty gasped. 'I didn't realise I was dealing with Stone Age man. You really do want the original barefoot bride, don't you?'

He attempted to put his arms around her, but she pulled violently away.

'Are you going to calm down?'

'Not in the immediate future,' she snapped truthfully.

'Then I'll turn into the surgery now and relieve Drew from holding the fort on his own.'

Beneath her incredulous scrutiny, he swept up his car keys. 'Do you know what's wrong with you? You've turned into one spoiled little madam. Whether you like it or not, I have commitments that extend beyond you and I can't always be here because you want me to be,' he drawled as if he were addressing a child in a temper tantrum.

Kitty was mutinously silent, impotently aware that her own secrecy had sent her up the creek without a paddle. Furthermore, if he didn't want a rich wife that was just too bad, he was getting one. All right, she would eventually have to tell him that Grant was her father, and she would have to tell him about the estate. There had to be a subtle method of breaking that last piece of news. Stunning him with a complete surprise package now seemed a very childish idea. He would be shattered, he night even be angry. But not for long, surely not for long?

Tina was trying to lug an attaché case up the stairs. 'I s'ought I should help,' she confided anxiously. 'Daddy slammed the front door. He must be tired.'

Jessie peered up at Kitty's flushed face from the hall below. 'He wasn't tired this morning,' she remarked flatly.

Kitty finished unpacking with Tina at her heels. When she went downstairs Jessie dealt her a weary glance. 'Are you ready to try on this dress. I've got to get it pressed.'

The older woman took her time over the final fitting, ignoring Kitty's strained mouth and drooping shoulders. When she had finished she shook her head reprovingly, effectively making Kitty feel about five years old again. 'I don't know why the two of you get on like that. It's not making you happy, is it?' she completed in a serves-you-right tone.

Merrill arrived at teatime to pick up Tina and Jessie went home. Kitty flicked through a magazine, tried to settle to the television and failed and ended up wandering aimlessly round the house. A line of family photographs in Sophie's formal drawing-room caught her attention. She studied them closely but neither Tina nor her mother featured.

Upstairs she picked up a shirt lying in Jake's room, and as her fingers creased the fabric the husky scent of his body drifted into her nostrils. She hugged the shirt, tears in her eyes, awash with emotion. She loved him, she loved him so much, and she wasn't prepared to do or say anything that might prevent their wedding taking place tomorrow.

In Tina's room she found what she had been most afraid to find—a silver-framed photograph on the dressing-table. It had to be Liz. A youthfully pretty female with dark blue eyes and pale blonde hair that

didn't look quite natural. She had a short upper lip tha
gave her a rather sulky pout even smiling.

'Kitty!' Startled, she hastily replaced the photo-fram
and hurried out on to the landing.

Jake was halfway up the stairs. 'I couldn't see a singl
light on at the front of the house!' The way he threw i
at her, the omission was an offence.

Perception leapt through her as she encountered the
charged onslaught of dark, intent eyes. You thought I'
gone. And you panicked. For a split second his capacity
to shield his thoughts from her was paper-thin. The hand
he had braced tautly on the wall dropped down to thrus
into the pocket of his trousers. His veiled gaze ran slowly
and very carefully over her. He breathed out and quirked
a brow. 'Did you wait up for me?'

'It is only ten.' She paused. 'Jessie left some suppe
for you.'

'I've already eaten. Would you like a drink?' he en
quired silkily. 'It might settle your nerves.'

'There's nothing the matter with my nerves,' she re
plied waspishly, and as quickly wished the tart word
unspoken. But Liz had a face now inside her head. Sh
was not so easy to forget.

Strong arms linked round her from behind. 'You'r
like a cat on hot bricks,' he contradicted gently.

'I don't like arguments,' she said tightly.

'I agree. Sane and civilised people sit down and discuss
things,' he murmured with level emphasis.

Pink stained her cheekbones. Finding his attentio
trained on her as if he could feel the troubled tenor o
her thoughts, she went round the lounge switching o
all the lamps when one would have done. 'I should hav
been more understanding about the hours you work,
she conceded very quietly.

Jake uncapped the brandy decanter on the polishe
sofa table and poured two measures. 'That wasn't th

bone of contention. I don't want anything Maxwell gave you in our lives and that includes the monetary value of anything you want to sell that he bought you. I don't see anything unreasonable in that,' he asserted with utter calm.

Kitty bent her head and clenched her teeth on an impulsive reply.

'Aside of that, you did make a very good point. Marriage is about sharing.' He passed her a glass. 'And there's absolutely nothing else that I don't want to share.'

'Was it like that with you and Liz?' she demanded abruptly.

He met her accusing gaze steadily. 'No, it wasn't.'

The silence lay. He added nothing more. His dark eyes were shuttered. He stared moodily into the fire. Kitty took a deep breath and broached the subject from another angle. 'Tell me, would you have taken her back if she hadn't been killed in that crash?'

'I don't know. I would have had to consider Tina, and Liz would have been quite capable of using her as a weapon,' he said grimly. 'Then I felt that the whole damned mess was my fault.'

'Why? Were you unfaithful as well?'

'No!' He thrust long fingers through his black hair in a gesture of raw frustration. 'I really don't want to discuss Liz with you at this moment. There are reasons...'

She didn't hear him. She was discovering that she could love him with a kind of mad, defiant desperation but that love didn't melt the hard little core of bitterness inside her. To generously forgive and forget was something she had still to learn how to do. How many men would even consider taking back an unfaithful wife, who had lived openly with her lover? Jake's generosity to Liz had been boundless. Kitty couldn't forget the agonies she had had to suffer alone—and all for what? For a woman he hadn't loved? A woman who no more than three years into their marriage had gone to bed with another man?

Really all along she had known the truth for herself, she registered in sick turmoil. Like a trusting child she had wanted to believe that he could ease that old bitter pain with some magic formula, but he had nothing new to tell her, nothing that she didn't already know. What fantasy castles had she built in the air? The truth was there before her as it had always been and she had to live with it.

Eight years ago he had struggled to be as honest with her as he had dared, but there really wasn't a kind way to tell a girl in love with you that you would be ashamed to take her out in public, that when other people entered the picture she would be an embarrassment. The wrong accent, the wrong clothes, the wrong background. Kitty was painfully conscious now of just how vast the gulf had been between them when she was a teenager. Aware of his scrutiny, she lifted her head. 'Does Tina have any relatives on her mother's side?'

'None. Liz's parents died before I met her. I'm expecting you to take on a ready-made family,' he said tautly. 'I realise that I'm asking a lot.'

Her lashes lowered. 'She's a very affectionate child. She won't be hard to love. Why doesn't your mother get on with her?'

'Sophie looks at Tina and sees Liz,' Jake proffered grimly. 'Liz's departure caused a lot of talk locally and Sophie has never forgotten that.'

'Not all women like children,' Kitty remarked.

He smiled at her, that beautiful blazing smile of his. 'I'd like us to have a child some time.'

Pallor spread over her locked facial muscles.

As he stared at her, his mouth compressed, his dark eyes shuttering. 'Or some time never,' he rephrased flatly. 'Since the idea appears to fill you with such horror.'

Regret and pain threatened to suffocate her in the silence. Once he had not even wanted to give her child a chance to be born. She didn't want to remember that, but it was one of those horrible, inescapable realities. And at that moment, it made her hate him as violently as she could love him.

'I'm afraid I don't want children,' she muttered jerkily and bent her head, exposing the vulnerable nape of her neck. 'And if things didn't work out between us, it will be better that way.'

'As a thought before the wedding, I find that pretty damned depressing,' he slashed back at her.

'I'm going to bed!' Leaping to her feet in one sudden motion, she brushed past him before he could glimpse the tears in her eyes.

The threat of seeing everything falling apart like a stack of cards built up too high had put her to flight. She couldn't sleep. She found that she could still cry for that tiny life she had lost. Yet the thought of Jake's baby inside her again was both a torment and a temptation.

If she was ever alone again, she didn't want to be left with nothing as she had been before. And should it happen, it would be so very different, she reflected feverishly in the darkness. She could live abroad. It would be silk-lined cribs and proper medical supervision all the way... dazedly she shook her head. Where were all these crazy ideas coming from?

There was something slightly unhinged about such reasoning when she was going to marry Jake. She loved him. My God, if she didn't love him, she would not have been afraid to voice her own feelings. Somehow she had to come to terms with this fear that could swoop down and swamp her without warning. It was a terror of being hurt again.

She was finally driven from her bed by the tormenting fears that found her an easy victim. It was four in the morning and the house was chilly. Rubbing her bare arms, she peered into Jake's room. The curtains were undrawn and the bed was smooth. He was stretched out asleep on the chesterfield in the lounge. Her conscience pricked her.

It was strange how the instant she saw him again all her tension could seep away. Just looking at Jake swept her with intense exultation. She had hurt him because, without realising it, he had hurt her. Lashing out in self-defence, she had retreated to lick her wounds in private. And he had done the same, neither of them able to reach out to the other. He didn't know why she had reacted as she had. And perhaps it was time that he did know, she accepted tautly. She wanted to let go of that old anguish and until she told him it would always be there, ready to feed her insecurity.

She fetched a blanket from upstairs. Draping the woolly thickness over his long, indolent length, she hesitated and then delicately sneaked under its warmth with him, tugging an arm possessively round her. As she twisted to rest her cheek in the hollow of a broad shoulder, his body scent enclosed her. Warm and husky and wonderfully familiar. She went out like a light within minutes.

A whisper of a kiss caressed her throat. She shifted, succumbing to an indulgent little wriggle of comfort. The hard, male physique beneath her relaxed weight tautened. 'Go back to sleep. It's still early.' The soothing whisper had a hypnotic effect on her.

When Jessie shook her awake she had a death-grip on a flattened pillow. As she sat up, amazed to find herself back in bed again, the housekeeper planted a tray on her lap and urged her to eat up. 'Jake insisted that I let you sleep until now, but it's almost nine,' she fussed. 'And Merrill's downstairs waiting for you to get up.'

Kitty gulped down a glass of pure orange. 'Where's Jake?'

'Out helping John to get cleared up. He's not coming up here,' Jessie warned. 'You can't see him until you arrive at the church.'

'How am I going to get there, then?'

'Merrill's taking us. I'll be going home afterwards,' Jessie informed her. 'You'll want to be on your own.'

Merrill presented her with an ivory lace suspender belt and brief set, complete with sheer lace-topped stockings. 'Jane sent them to me at Christmas but they're about two sizes too small for me.' She grinned. 'And even if they weren't, that sort of thing's not really me ... but it's definitely my brother.'

An hour later Kitty twirled in front of the mirror. Great-grandma Tarrant's gown was a ravishingly romantic confection. Watermarked Mantua silk shimmered beneath a fragile, floaty drapery of cream lace. Kitty was entranced.

Jessie removed her pinny to reveal an imposing purple wool suit and draped a fur coat, purloined from Sophie's bedroom, round Kitty's shoulders. 'You'll catch your death otherwise,' she grumbled.

Tina thrust a handful of somewhat mangled crocuses wrapped in tin foil into her hand. 'They're from the window-box. Some of them got broked,' she said apologetically.

'What a lovely colour they are. See, they match my dress,' Kitty commented cheerfully.

The vicar greeted her punctiliously in the church porch. At the mouth of the short aisle, her knees threatened to buckle when an unseen organist loudly struck up a piece from 'Lohengrin'. Oh, dear God, what am I doing? flashed through her mind, and then her bemused eyes centred on Jake's tall, elegant back view and that was it. Only the vicar's restraining pace prevented her from arriving at the altar before him.

Apart from one brief manic inner vision of Sophie and Grant popping up like evil genies from a back pew to halt the proceedings, Kitty was possessed of a euphoric brand of tranquillity throughout the ceremony. As the last syllables were pronounced, Jake swung round and engulfed her in the kind of embrace she had never anticipated experiencing on church ground. His arm a steel band across her narrow back, he crushed her fiercely to him and ravished her soft lips until the blood sang in her veins.

'If they ever do a remake of *Gone with the Wind*, Jake,' his sister whispered in the vestry, 'ask for an audition.'

A stocky, brown-haired man shook Kitty's hand and introduced himself as John. Until that moment Kitty hadn't even registered him, and his amused look told her that he had noticed the fact.

They were invited back to the other couple's home for a celebratory drink. Although their modern bungalow had its own entrance off the main road, it was connected to Torbeck as well by a lane. As soon as Kitty had a glass in her hand, Merrill bore her off on a tour of the house. She chattered constantly, but gave Kitty little opportunity to comment. By the time they reached the nursery, already prepared for the expected baby, Kitty was covertly studying Merrill, puzzled by her perceptible nervous tension.

A brief silence fell as Kitty smoothed an admiring hand over a patchwork cot quilt and her sister-in-law chose that moment to break into sudden speech.

'I hope I'm not about to offend you, but I wanted a private word with you about Mother.' Stopping to draw breath, she pressed on as if afraid that Kitty would interrupt her. 'She's worried that your marriage will cut

her off completely from Jake. They don't get on very
well as it is.'

'I had gathered that.' Kitty's tone was non-committal.

Merrill sighed. 'It's been like that for years. On Jake's
side, not hers. She has interfered now and again in his
private life and Jake's not the type to take that lying
down. But you can't blame her for loathing Liz!' She
defended her absent parent with growing heat. 'After all
this time, I do think that Jake could let bygones be
bygones.'

'I'm not in a position to comment,' Kitty murmured.
'I assume your mother's upset about our marriage.'

'Actually it almost seems to have frightened her,'
Merrill confided unhappily. 'Jake said that they didn't
argue when he visited her in York, but I don't believe
him. He's incredibly touchy about you. If Mother did
say something tactless, he would have lost his temper.
She sounded very shaken up when she phoned me last
night. She said that she would be coming back in a few
days. She wants to meet you here in our house...'

'Here?' Kitty exclaimed blankly. 'But why?'

'I think she wants to make her peace with you and
she doesn't want to have to do it with Jake smouldering
suspiciously on the sidelines.'

'But your mother doesn't have anything to make peace
with me about,' Kitty retorted wryly.

'She must just want to talk to you, then.' Merrill
chewed her lower lip awkwardly. 'I wanted to ask you
to be generous. If you could meet her halfway and try
to smooth things over between her and Jake, I'd be very
grateful. She really was distressed on the phone. You
could reason with Jake. You have more influence with
him than anyone else.'

Before Kitty could remark on that assurance and its
attendant weight of shifted responsibility, the door
opened, disclosing her new husband. Jake favoured her

with a dark, satirical smile. 'Don't tell me you became engrossed in the merits of alphabet wallpaper.'

Having stated her case, Merrill was clearly not sorry for the interruption and she laughed. 'Have you been feeling neglected?'

In the car Jake loosened his tie and cast Kitty a questioning glance. 'Since the prospect of the patter of little tiny feet leaves you cold as charity, what were you talking about?'

Searing pink burnished her cheekbones. She bent her head guiltily. Why had she lied to him like that? They would have to talk soon. She would have to tell him everything. But not today, she pleaded with her conscience. She couldn't face dredging up a past she wanted to forget on a day when she wanted to do nothing but luxuriate in her happiness. 'Nothing important.'

'I'm glad that you and Merrill hit it off.'

'I get on with most people.' Pausing, she added impulsively, 'I think I could even get on with your mother, given a chance.'

His dark gaze glittered. 'So Merrill was playing devil's advocate. She doesn't have a clue what she's talking about. Oh, you'll be given your chance,' he acknowledged abrasively. 'But I'll be very surprised if you emerge from the encounter feeling as generous as you feel now.'

His cynical response made her feel foolish. Sophie must have been very unpleasant about her. No doubt his mother wanted to see her at Merrill's solely to have an opportunity to attack, but Kitty refused to let that daunting prospect detract from her buoyant mood.

Back at Torbeck, Jake swept her into his arms, hungry dark eyes skimming possessively over her upturned face. 'How does it feel to be Mrs Tarrant?'

'You're still on trial,' she said unsteadily.

'It's going to be good . . . hell! It's going to be perfect,' he promised, feathering his lips fleetingly across her smooth forehead.

Her hands clutched convulsively at the lapels of his charcoal-grey jacket before diving into the depths of his black hair, seeking to bring his dark head down to hers. He resisted the pressure. 'Patience is a virtue,' he drawled mockingly as he carried her up the stairs.

'I don't seem to have it.' Her chagrined mutter roused his amusement, but, as he lowered her with intoxicating slowness down the length of his body, he kissed her breathless and the world spun. Her feet touched the bedroom carpet and she wasn't aware of it. An irresistible passion had taken control of her.

His hands roamed over her back, gliding down to cup her hips and ease her even closer to the stirring hardness between his thighs. His tongue delved a possession that wildly inflamed her senses. As his deft fingers released the last pearl button at the base of her spine, air cooled her hot skin. He stepped back, heedless of her instinctive cry of protest and tugged the narrow sleeves down her arms in a calm unhurried movement.

The gown pooled in a lacy tangle at her toes. In the act of bending to free her of the construction, he stilled and straightened, arrested by the scraps of silk which embellished her porcelain-pale skin. As his rich dark eyes devoured her, enchanting colour lent definition to her face.

'A gift from your sister,' she muttered uncertainly.

'My compliments to Merrill, but I really didn't need this encouragement.' His mouth tilted appreciatively and he extended a hand. 'Come here,' he invited with husky impatience.

She must have made that step, but later she didn't remember it. Her shy attempts to divest him of his shirt were brought to a halt by the explosive demand of his mouth. Lifting her, he laid her on the bed and moved back to strip off his own clothing with a marked lack of ceremony. Her silk adornments met with similar disrespect, tossed carelessly aside as he knelt over her, dark and magnificent in his virile arousal.

His head lowered to suckle at her taut nipples, his hand travelling over her quivering stomach to a more intimate destination. Discovering her readiness, he bore her back with a harsh groan of satisfaction and thrust urgently into her. She arched in joyous welcome to his driving possession, abandoning herself to the passionate joining of their bodies. He filled her with his warmth at the peak of the highest plateau and she felt more complete than she had ever felt in her life before.

Satiated, she smoothed his damp hair, pressed her mouth spontaneously to the fingertips that tenderly stroked across her cheek. As she lay there, the secret she had zealously maintained from him niggled briefly at the outer edges of her contentment. To admit that for her there was no other man, indeed that in all this time there had never been another man...she frowned. It would be to tell him too much. Such honesty would carry with it the confession of love, and she wasn't prepared to admit her own weakness when it wasn't his. She crushed the little voice drily asking how long she could possibly keep such a secret. This obviously wasn't the right moment—perhaps in another few days, she thought fleetingly, unconsciously ducking the issue yet again.

Later they tucked into a casserole which Jessie had with sound sense left in the fridge.

'For somebody writing a book, you're remarkably quiet about it,' Jake breathed mockingly. 'Aren't you going to tell me what it's about?'

'It's a murder mystery,' Kitty conceded with reluctance.

'A murder mystery?' Lounging back indolently in his chair, he surveyed her with unconcealed amusement. 'If you had allowed me one guess, I would have said historical with a dash of romance.'

'You did have one guess,' she reminded him stiffly, for the memory still rankled.

'To get beyond the first chapter on that topic, you really would have had to let your imagination run riot.' He gave her a slumbrous smile. 'When can I read it?'

Heat suffusing her complexion, she got up to clear the table. 'I haven't written much of it yet.'

His dark scrutiny gleamed with humour. 'My powers of concentration were equally shot until I decided to corner and coerce you into giving me a second chance.'

'Is that what you did?'

He reached for her suddenly and pulled her down on to his thighs to bury his mouth in the fragrant veil of her hair. 'I'll never give you cause to regret it,' he muttered with rough sincerity.

Somewhere in the night she surfaced bemusedly to discover that Jake had deliberately kissed her awake. She curved into him and clung. With a husky sound of satisfaction, he swept her into a world of passionate oblivion.

In the morning she woke alone and it panicked her. Flying downstairs she found Jessie busily vacuuming the lounge. The older woman straightened. 'He's out on a call to the estate. He was in no mood to go, but Drew's off somewhere else. And Merrill phoned,' she completed wryly.

'Merrill?'

'To ask if you would come over and see Tina this morning,' Jessie filled in. 'I don't see why. You only saw the child yesterday.'

'Maybe she's upset about something,' Kitty murmured worriedly.

After a snatched breakfast, only eaten at Jessie's insistence, she decided to walk over to Merrill's. It was a beautiful, fresh morning. The sunlight warmed her skin with the promise of spring in the air.

An unfamiliar red car was parked outside the bungalow and Kitty hesitated before she rang the bell, wondering if she should have phoned before setting out.

Merrill answered the door with anxious eyes and an apologetic smile. 'I'm really sorry. I wouldn't have rung today if she hadn't insisted, but I wasn't expecting her to come back this soon,' she volunteered in a rush. 'I didn't know what to do and then I saw Jake driving off...'

A frown of incomprehension had marred Kitty's brow. 'I'm afraid I don't know——'

'Mother's here,' Merrill framed reluctantly. 'She's in the lounge.'

Kitty froze. 'Your mother? But——'

'Look, I'm going to pick up Tina from playgroup and then I'm popping into a friend's for an hour,' Merrill confided, hurriedly removing her coat from the cloakroom. 'That should give you plenty of time to chat in peace.'

Merrill gave her an uneasy look and then walked out of the house and climbed into her car. Kitty took a deep, sustaining breath before entering the lounge with what she hoped was a composed smile. A tall, gaunt woman with champagne-tinted hair and a tight mouth turned stiffly from the window. Sophie's thin, lined features had not worn well. The svelte, still attractive blonde whom Kitty remembered had gone. This woman looked more than her sixty years.

'Won't you sit down?' Sophie made the suggestion brittly. 'I had to persuade Merrill to go out. I couldn't risk her overhearing what I have to say to you.'

The ominous assurance provoked a wry glance from Kitty as she took a reluctant seat. 'Then wouldn't it be better not to say whatever it is?'

'Do you think I wanted this meeting? Do you think I had any choice?' Sophie dealt her a look that was a curious mixture of dislike and desperation. 'I knew you were at Lower Ridge before I left. That's why I went to my sister's. I didn't want to be here when you told Jake, but you still hadn't told him when he came to see me...so perhaps I'm not too late after all.'

Kitty had the uncomfortable sensation that she was dealing with someone not quite in possession of all their faculties. Her attention lingered on the nervous twitch of Sophie's hands as she clasped them together. 'I'm sorry. I don't understand. What didn't you want me to tell Jake?'

'If you tell him that you were pregnant when he married Liz, he'll blame me for that as well!' Sophie condemned in a sudden rush. 'And I won't have that. Do you hear me? I won't have it. You've caused enough trouble!'

Shock had dilated Kitty's eyes. She turned her head away sharply to conceal her distress, a sense of bitter humiliation assailing her. 'How did you find out?' she asked when she had herself under control again.

'Your grandmother told me, but it was too late. He was already married. I offered her money but she wouldn't take it,' Sophie volunteered defensively. 'I didn't tell Jake. Of course I didn't. Good God, I never thought you'd come back here!'

Kitty bent her head, unwilling to look at her.

'What happened to the baby?' Sophie demanded in a curt undertone. 'Did you have it adopted?' and then more loudly, 'I suppose you got rid of it once you got away from those old people!'

Kitty shut her eyes in mute distaste, wishing she could as efficiently shut out that ranting, hysterically shrill voice. 'I had a miscarriage.'

'That horrible old woman!' Sophie gasped. 'All these years. She should have told me instead of leaving me in ignorance.'

Since her concern hadn't led her to visit Martha Colgan and ask, Kitty didn't take the hint that Sophie had endured a sleepless night or two very seriously. 'You said that Jake would blame you,' she reminded her stiffly. 'I don't see why. I don't even understand why we should discuss this. It all happened a very long time ago.'

Sophie's pale blue eyes centred on her vindictively. 'It wasn't his baby, was it?' she stabbed with offensive pleasure.

Kitty looked steadily back at her, unsurprised by the vicious attack. 'It was. So I wouldn't hurry to tell Jake otherwise.'

Sophie's bright scrutiny dulled and she turned back to the window, her abrupt movements betraying that she was still in a very emotional state. 'Did you know that your mother once worked in the estate office?'

'My mother?' Completely thrown once more by the peculiar change of subject, Kitty stared at her. 'No, I didn't know that.'

'Jake was only two years old,' Sophie continued tight-lipped. 'I still had all my illusions intact about my marriage. It took your mother to disenchant me. Charles made a fool of himself over her.'

Kitty's brows had knitted. 'I don't quite follow,' she said, although she was terribly afraid that she did.

'Don't you? He wouldn't leave her alone,' Sophie rephrased in disgust. 'Now I believe they call it sexual harassment. He was more than twice her age, old enough to know better! Your mother was very shocked by his behaviour.'

'What happened?' Kitty murmured uneasily.

Sophie loosed a choked laugh. 'She handed in her notice. I will never forget the look of pity in her eyes when she told me that she was leaving. She felt sorry for me!' she vented shrilly. 'I despised her for it.'

'But if she didn't encourage your husband——'

'Do you really believe that that made it any less humiliating for me?' Sophie demanded. 'Do you think other people didn't notice how he was behaving? Your mother made a laughing stock of me. There were those who said there was no smoke without fire. I was glad when she had to leave home to find another job.'

In other words, her mother had suffered for something that was not her fault, Kitty reflected grimly. Impatience nipped at her. Sophie had imparted her sense of injury at great enough depth. Kitty had grasped that the older woman had transferred her loathing for her late mother to her, but she saw no reason for a lengthy discussion about a non-event that had occurred before she was even born.

'I think we ought to concentrate on the present, Mrs Tarrant,' she said gently, for unless she was very much mistaken Sophie had her back turned to her now because she was in tears.

She jerked round. 'If only it were that simple,' she muttered shakily. 'You won't believe me, but I didn't really dislike you when you were a child. You didn't harm me. It seemed like poetic justice when you fell in love with my son. I didn't care because I didn't think he was in any real danger. After all, I'd done everything I could to make him see that you could never fit into our lives, and I thought I had succeeded until I saw him kissing you at our last New Year party. I was appalled but I blamed you for it!'

'Yes,' Kitty said, wondering when Sophie's ramblings would begin to make sense.

Mrs Tarrant's face contorted with bitterness. 'Believe me, it was a ghastly enough evening without that. Everybody wanted to know where Charles was and I couldn't tell them. He'd said that he wanted a divorce but I didn't realise he meant it until he failed to come home for the party. The last thing I needed that evening was to see you in my son's arms.'

Compassion had touched Kitty in an unexpected surge. She screened her eyes, aware that sympathy would not be welcome. Sophie sank down almost clumsily in the seat opposite and pressed a hanky to her trembling mouth. 'I thought I knew my son and I didn't. I thought it was an infatuation he would soon get over. I believed that you had encouraged him to behave that way, but you must accept,' she whispered with a slight sob catching at her voice, 'I never dreamt that he might have slept with you or that you could be pregnant. I knew he wouldn't listen to me if I told him to stay away from you. So I had to tell him something that would make him stay away. It was for his own good. I did it for him...'

'What did you do for him?' Kitty muttered tautly, finally realising that Mrs Tarrant was finding it very difficult to come to the point.

'All I wanted to do was knock any foolish ideas he might have about you right out of his head. I was determined to stop it going one step further,' Sophie confessed tearfully. 'Nobody knew who your father was and I didn't care that I had to lie. I knew it wouldn't go any further. I told Jake that you had the same father. I told him that you were his half-sister...'

Kitty's heartbeat had lodged suffocatingly in her throat. In sick horror and disbelief she stared at the older woman, but Sophie wouldn't meet her eyes.

'I also knew that if Jake approached Charles he would deny it. But my husband would have denied anything like that. I knew that Jake would still believe me,' she asserted, tearing at her hanky with restive fingers and then sobbing accusingly at Kitty, 'I did it for him, and then he went off and married that little tart because he couldn't have you!'

Kitty had sustained such a shock that Sophie had swum out of focus. 'And he actually believed you?' she mumbled in nauseated turmoil.

'Yes. I made it a good story with plenty of details,' Sophie admitted without remorse, drying her eyes, calming now that she had reached her climax. 'I convinced him.'

'And when did you tell him the truth?' Kitty demanded with sudden ferocity.

'When I was ill. I didn't mean to tell him. I was never going to tell him but somehow I did.' She cast Kitty a glance of barely concealed hatred. 'He accused me of ruining his life. If it weren't for you, my son and I would still be close.'

Waxen-pale, Kitty murmured, 'Why didn't Jake tell me all this?'

Sophie tautened. 'When he came to my sister's I begged him not to tell you. I persuaded him that it was only fair to let me explain. I made him promise me.'

'Because you were afraid that I'd mention the baby.' The syllables hurt Kitty's aching throat.

'Why should you tell him?' Sophie snapped. 'You've got him now. Can't you be satisfied with that? I'm the one who has suffered.'

Kitty stood up, too dazed to feel anger, too shaken to want more than to escape Sophie's venomous presence. She had spun an unforgivable web of lies and she wasn't particularly sorry that she had done so. Kitty didn't believe that, at the time, Sophie had cared very much more about how those lies affected her son. Her most powerful motivation had been to ensure that Jake put Kitty out

of his life, and the depths she had sunk to in obtaining
that end suggested to Kitty that Sophie had been pun
ishing her son for daring to go against her.

'I suppose you weren't well at the time,' Kitty allowed
painfully. 'But don't blame me for causing trouble be
tween you and Jake. That, at least, can't be laid at my
door.'

CHAPTER TEN

KITTY turned off the lane to walk through the fields. All those lives affected, all that suffering, she reflected in a stupor. Jake had loved her and his mother had made that love a forbidden emotion to be suppressed and denied. On the brink of losing her husband, Sophie had fought not to lose her son as well. What a farce it must have been when Jake had gone off at a tangent and married someone else! His mother hadn't planned for that eventuality.

The wind stung her wet cheeks. She was crying. How much had he loved her? If Sophie hadn't interfered, what would have happened between them? Would he have wanted her child? Would he have asked her to marry him? Or had his mother's lies supplied him with an unpalatable but not unwelcome escape route from an extremely difficult situation?

She walked all the way to Lower Ridge. She didn't want to see anyone until she had regained her equilibrium. The cottage was a blackened shell with gaping windows. Sophie, she registered painfully, had changed the entire course of her life. Eight years ago, Jake would have married her—whether he'd wanted to or not. He would have married her because she'd been carrying his child. And his mother and his sisters would have made her life hell behind his back.

Her father had been ashamed of her as she had been then. Would Jake have been the same? Jake, whose manners were so ingrained that they were second nature to him, Jake, who had never known what it was to feel

self-conscious in any kind of company...Jake. Sud
denly she needed him with a violent intensity that shud
dered through her.

What on earth was she doing here? She was her own
worst enemy. What was the point in these agonised
thoughts of what might have been? She started home
There was so much she wanted to tell him now, so much
she needed to ask. The Range Rover was in the yard
parked at an angle as if Jake had vacated it in a hurry
Delighted that he was back, she pushed through the back
door. Tugging off her muddy boots, she sniffed appreciatively. The kitchen was tantalisingly full of the
smell of roast lamb. She could hear Jessie vacuuming
upstairs.

Jake intercepted her in the hall. 'Where the hell have
you been?'

'Merrill's,' she answered in bewilderment.

His dark features rigid with anger, he clamped a steel-
fingered hand to her arm and pressed her into the lounge,
slamming the door shut behind them. He didn't know
his own strength. She massaged her benumbed forearm
with unsteady fingers, her eyes wide. 'What's wrong?'

He faced her with his long, straight legs braced slightly
apart. Aggression wrote high-wire tension into every lean,
sinuous line of his body. As dark, intent eyes settled
fiercely on her, her heartbeat speeded up, a lurch of
fearful apprehension filling her.

'Bob Creighton's boss was up at the Grange yesterday
with a surveying team. Apparently Barker let your name
slip in conversation and then tried to swear Creighton
to secrecy.'

In the throbbing silence, a surge of guilty crimson
slowly stained her cheekbones. Her eyes fell from his.

'My God,' he whispered in a seething undertone. 'It's
true. You're behind Colwell Holdings. You own the
estate!'

Her teeth had drawn blood from her lower lip. 'I didn't want you to find out like this. I was going to . . . surprise you . . .'

'Surprise me? You wanted to surprise me with the news that you thought you could buy and sell me ten times over?' His raw incredulity sliced into her like a physical blow.

'Who told you?'

'Creighton. The man is worried about the security of his job. He approached me. Word of our marriage has leaked out locally. Creighton seemed to think that I would be taking over the estate. I could put my hands round that scrawny, lying little throat of yours and squeeze hard!' he swore with sudden savagery. 'Everything you've done since you came back here has been based on lies and duplicity. But God, did you need to go to such lengths to make a fool of me?'

'I didn't! I didn't know how to tell you!' she gasped, devastated by the suspicions he had about her motive for silence. 'It's your home, Jake, and I want it to be ours. I just want you to have it back!'

'You want me to have it back. And you actually believed that I would accept it?' he demanded, his dangerously quiet inflexion fracturing with the charge of his anger. 'It didn't occur to you that I might have some reservations about living off the proceeds of immoral earnings?'

'W . . . what?' Her swimming violet eyes were fixed pleadingly to him. Her brain was functioning in slow motion. Mrs Tarrant had left her feeling weak and vulnerable.

'Col—well. Colgan-Maxwell,' he spelt out with derisive bite. 'He did indeed pay generously for his pleasure. I can hardly believe that you ceded me the same privileges without a price-tag attached! You've got the principles of a whore, Kitty. And I will tell you now that I am not living with them.'

Ashen pale, she protested, 'Jake, you have to listen to me. This has gone far enough. Grant's not my——'

A graphic expletive cut her off mid-speech. 'Do you really think that I care any more whether he is past or present? I told you how I felt last week. You can take your ill-gotten gains out of this house and march that little carcass of yours up the road to the Grange, but you will go alone!'

'I might just do that!' she threatened wildly.

He wrenched open the door with a flourish. 'Go ahead, and while you're up there have the grace to recall some of the elementary manners I instilled in you. Apologise to your manager. Employees deserve a little respect and consideration.'

'You swine!' she sobbed. 'It would serve you right if I did leave you!'

She fled upstairs, almost toppling the vacuum cleaner on the landing. The crash of the bedroom door reverberated through the entire house as she flung herself across the bed.

A minute later the door swung wide.

'I wish I'd never married you!' she threw at him painfully.

'And I'd like to know why you did. Was it one big ego trip? You didn't marry me for any of the usual reasons. You don't need security and you don't want children. Couldn't you resist the appeal of falling between the sheets with someone younger and more virile?' he shot at her fiercely. 'Am I that hot in bed?'

Her eyes stung. He towered over her where she lay. Tall and dark and very, very still. As he studied her prone body, an odd little chill ran over her. 'I meant what I said a few days ago,' he delivered harshly.

She was choking on a volatile mix of rage and savaged pride and pain. 'You weren't so particular last night!'

He dug a long-fingered hand into his pocket. A handful of notes fluttered down on the bed. 'I'm sorry. I don't know the going rate,' he said insolently softly. 'But I wouldn't want you to feel that I appreciated your beautiful body less than Maxwell. But then he wasn't over-scrupulous, was he? Why the hell should I be?'

He flayed her skin from her bones and tore her heart from its moorings. She clashed sickly with glittering eyes that had not a shred of compassion. As she attempted to scramble off the bed, he caught her with powerful hands and pinned her flat. 'This appears to be the only avenue of communication which you recognise,' he intoned hardly. 'And we are about to communicate.'

'Don't you dare!' she gasped.

'I thought the relationship between sex and money was the biggest addiction you had. But you made one cardinal error. I'm not for sale,' he grated. 'This is the last move in the game, Kitty. And it is mine. It's too bad you're not the shining prize I thought you were.'

With every harsh syllable he heaped humiliation on her. She shuddered, she bled from that final brutal indictment. He was rejecting her. That he could still desire her was merely another subtle and cruel way to weight the punishment. Rejection was an old friend to her. She had feared and anticipated it. Subconsciously she had been waiting for this moment, this torment from the beginning, and it was not within her power to fight those feelings.

But still her body burned when he touched her. It did not differentiate between anger and passion. He stormed her defences and she was too weak to deny him. The brilliance of a falling star blinded her and then there was nothing. Less than nothing. And she was lost somewhere in the terrifying emptiness that was swallowing her up.

She pretended to be asleep until he left. A bank-note lay crumpled beneath her rigid fingers as she raised herself. She crawled upright on hollow legs and all that drove her was an overpowering need to be gone before he returned. She threw a few handfuls of clothes pell-mell into a single case.

'What on earth are you doing?' Jessie whispered from the doorway.

'I'm leaving.' Kitty's voice sounded far away to her.

'You've had an argument and his temper got the better of him, but whatever he said he won't have meant it,' Jessie argued in desperation. 'He asked me if I knew about the estate. I think he was praying that it was all a misunderstanding. Why didn't you tell him, Kitty? You've run up against that pride of his and he's raw with it.'

Jessie's voice was an intrusive drone in Kitty's ears. She gave the older woman a blank look from dulled, dead eyes as she closed her case with trembling hands. She was adrift on a sea of all-encompassing pain. Jake had hurt her when she was at her most loving and giving. Jake despised her. Jake had shown her that she was nothing more than a body from which he could extract only a physical and transient fulfilment.

Jessie was still talking to her when she climbed into her car and she still wasn't relating to a single thing she said. It was late evening before she arrived in London. Mrs Stuart accepted her arrival without comment. After fifteen years in Grant's employment, his housekeeper had developed an almost robotic air of detachment to the various events that disturbed the peace of the household she ran so efficiently.

In the exquisitely furnished familiarity of her own suite of rooms, the rigid discipline Kitty had imposed on herself for hundreds of miles collapsed. But there was no release in tears. She was engulfed by a depression, blacker and more frightening than anything she had ever known. The following day passed without her noticing it. She didn't eat from the trays that appeared and she didn't sleep in her bed.

That evening Mrs Stuart came to speak to her. 'Mr Maxwell has arranged for you to fly out to France tomorrow afternoon, Miss Colgan.'

Kitty frowned. 'How did he know I was here?'

'Mr Maxwell's secretary telephoned this morning,' Mrs Stuart divulged, neglecting to add that Becky had phoned every day at her employer's request to find out whether or not Kitty had arrived.

Grant met her at Nice airport. A tall, slimly built man, who kept himself in the physical peak of condition, he had sun-streaked blond hair and the same cheekbones that lent such definition to his daughter's face. Kitty experienced a split second of joyous recognition and then it all went wrong.

They were mobbed by his faithful fans and an aggressive contingent of paparazzi. As the suffocating crush of human bodies was held at bay by Grant's security guards, Kitty was at screaming-point. She was painfully convinced that she had just received yet another polished paternal demonstration of how to manipulate the publicity machine to one's own advantage.

With remarkable forbearance, her father neglected to comment on her bruised eyes, her pallor and her fined-down features. Unperturbed by her monosyllabic responses, he managed to have an entire conversation with himself in the rear of the limousine that ferried them to the villa where he was staying.

The palatial building, loaned to him by a close friend, was secreted behind high walls and electronic gates. In a vast tiled hall with a soaring ceiling and the acoustics of Westminster Cathedral, he took gross insensitivity to new heights.

'You'll want to freshen up before we go out to dinner,' he told her in a rallying tone. 'We're eating out at La Chevre d'Or. A gastronomic experience *par excellence*.'

Under her despairing gaze, he kissed his fingertips French fashion. 'And it will be a dinner you will never forget,' an unfamiliar voice promised sweetly from the top of the stairs.

Grant whipped round, his charismatic smile evaporating with almost comical suddenness. 'What are you doing here?' he snapped.

A lush brunette, clad in ice-blue separates, was calmly descending the stairs, secure in the knowledge that she held the floor. Kitty recognised her instantly. Grant's co-star, Yolanda Simons.

'I made the booking at La Chevre D'Or,' Yolanda announced, directing a killing smile at Kitty. 'I should warn you that you will be sharing your table with a third party—namely me. I'm not prepared to be publicly ditched during the making of this film. Do stop scowling like that, Grant. You look like a cross little boy. You should understand that this is a matter of image. It is not personal.'

Kitty shot her flushed father a disgusted glance. 'Tell her.'

'Tell her what?' He employed volume and voice pitch to intimidate.

Kitty was beyond intimidation. 'Grant is my father, Miss Simons. I am his daughter. I am not a rival. And I do not have any plans to spoil your dinner engagement this evening. I shall be eating in.'

For the count of five seconds, Yolanda's sultry mouth was wide. Kitty didn't dare look at her father. She continued on up the stairs in the wake of her luggage.

'Your daughter? Your daughter!' Yolanda was shrieking in a rage. 'And you let me think...'

Grant was receiving his just deserts. Kitty stifled a pang of conscience as she heard him trying to bluster loudly out of the confrontation. She had done something she should have done years ago. She had forced the issue, and now that the skeleton was out of the closet it would eventually rattle its bones in the outside world.

A maid arrived to do her unpacking. Dismissing her, Kitty continued to pace the floor. She expected her father to blaze explosively into her presence at any moment. When he failed to appear, she wondered if he was taking Yolanda out to dinner after all. She was well acquainted with her parent's astonishing ability to charm the angriest females into purring complacency.

At eleven she abandoned her strained vigil and crawled into her elegant Empire bed to stare miserably up at the ceiling. As the turbulence of her emotions emerged from the stultifying fog of self-pity, doubts cast her into turmoil.

Jake had run over her like a truck. But hadn't she connived at her own downfall? Candour would have resolved the conflict between them. What she was struggling to come to terms with now was that, even in the midst of that violent argument, she had made no real attempt to tell him the truth about Grant.

It had been so easy to tell Yolanda, but she had withheld it from the man she loved. Jealousy had twisted Jake's view of her with disastrous consequences. She had kept quiet, stubbornly and stupidly using the most divisive and combustible emotion in existence as a subversive weapon. Jake had retaliated and she had bolted, something he had once suggested she did all too easily.

When those pictures of her with Grant hit the papers, their separation would be permanent. She fought a sensation that came very close to pure panic and an aching

tide of longing for Jake could not be put to flight. She
was remembering how supportive and kind he had been
in spite of her insults when she had first arrived at Lower
Ridge. And by the time she worked through to remembering how he had plunged into a burning house to save
her life, she was crying her heart out so she didn't hear
the knock on the door.

'I saw your light on . . . God,' Grant groaned as she
twisted away to wipe clumsily at her tear-swollen face.
'This takes me back eight years to a phase I don't want
to live through with you again.'

Gulping she sat up and was nonplussed. He didn't look
furious. He didn't walk in a very straight line either,
which shook her. A devotee to the cult of the body beautiful, Grant usually stuck to mineral waters. He had a
large brandy in his hands as he lowered himself down
into an armchair by the bed. 'I was planning to make a
Press release about us when I finished the film,' he informed her.

'Were you?'

Meeting drenched violet eyes, he sighed, 'Well, I was
thinking about it. I don't know why I let the charade go
on for so long. No, that's a lie. It amused me.'

Unaccustomed to her father in a morose mood, she
forced a smile. 'Did you soothe Yolanda?'

'She didn't need to be soothed. She went out of here
laughing like a drain,' he related humourlessly. 'I spent
the evening dreaming up a Press release about my long-
lost daughter. I hope you're not looking for recog-
nisable facts. There aren't any. I let your mother down
badly. I am fifty-two years old tomorrow and you are
the only person in my life whom I have ever really cared
about. Some track record that, isn't it?'

'Fifty-two?' she couldn't help parroting.

He winced. 'Fifty-two.' He rolled his brandy round
the glass slowly. 'I thought I was being tactful earlier,

but now I'll be blunt. Tell me about him. I hate the bastard, but who needs an open mind at a wake?'

She swallowed chokily. 'I don't want to bore you.'

'Take my mind off my birthday,' he invited gloomily.

She started at the beginning and then leap-frogged back and forth. He phoned down for a bottle of brandy and another glass. She glossed so fast over the wedding, he almost missed out on it. When she mentioned the fire, he looked at her in horror and loosed a pungent remark about it being very kind of her to have kept him informed. When silence finally fell, her father was surveying her more cheerfully and she was in tears again. 'At least he's not after your money.'

Aghast, she stared at him. 'Is that all you've got to say?'

'It springs to mind that Romeo and Juliet hit on the perfect solution, but don't take that as a serious piece of advice,' he quipped. 'Why the blazes didn't you admit that I was your father? You really put him through the wringer. And in my name too. Now I've got him on my conscience as well. That is all I required to make my cup truly overflow.'

The internal phone buzzed. Grant stretched out a long arm to answer it. His frown of impatience slowly faded to be replaced by an expression of growing amusement. Involved in diving for another issue, Kitty didn't follow one word in five of her father's fast and fluent French.

'Do something with your face,' he said abruptly. 'You've turned blotchy.'

Hurt, she wriggled off the bed and vanished into the en-suite bathroom. Cool water eased her hot, stretched skin. She tugged a comb through her tossed hair and returned to the bedroom.

'Assuming that he takes the stairs at a normal pace, your husband is going to walk through that door in about three minutes,' Grant imparted.

'P . . . pardon?' she stammered.

'He pinned the security guard on the gate to the wall and forced him to use the phone.' Her father's eyes gleamed with rich appreciation. 'It doesn't take Sherlock Holmes to deduce that Jake has come to snatch you from your den of iniquity and wipe the floor with me. I wouldn't miss this for the world.'

'Jake's here?' In consternation, Kitty leapt back off the bed.

No knock gave forewarning of Jake's precipitate entry. He came through the door and froze in his tracks, night-dark eyes whipping from Kitty's stilled figure to the man standing on the other side of the room. Her eyes clung to his lithe, taut physique in close-fitting jeans and a leather blouson jacket. Her mouth ran dry and a wave of weakness swept her.

What Grant read in Jake's unshielded eyes more than satisfied him. 'Before you get the wrong idea——' he began.

'She belongs with me and I'm taking her home,' Jake interposed harshly. 'But before I leave, I intend to——'

'I'm Kitty's father,' Grant cut in.

A muscle jerked at the edge of Jake's hard-set mouth, his scrutiny impassive. Grant grimaced. 'Maybe I flatter myself, but there's a distinct resemblance. It's always amazed me that nobody has ever noticed it.'

'It's true.' Her tongue finally unglued from the roof of her mouth. 'He is my father.'

'And I'm going public tomorrow,' Grant added. 'We can get acquainted some other time when you've had the time to face the depressing prospect of our all being one family. *Ciao*, children. You can battle for the rest of the night if you like, but I'm for my bed.'

He strolled out of the door under Jake's dazed stare. His dark head spun back, dark eyes flaming over her. 'You're his daughter? How the hell is that possible?'

She swallowed hard. 'My mother was working as a hotel receptionist when she met him. He wasn't famous then. He was with a repertory company that was touring the north. He persuaded her to return to London with him,' she explained against a background of absolute silence that was uniquely discouraging. 'He was offered a part in a television series in New York. He left her in London. He promised he would send her the money to join him. But he didn't.'

'Tell me something that's a surprise.' Jake snatched up the bottle of brandy and poured a measure into the glass she hadn't touched. He raised it almost clumsily to his lips and threw it back. His clenched profile sent further arrows of alarm stabbing into her.

'He's always insisted that he did write to her, but I don't think he did. When my mother decided to go home, she was pregnant, and she must have been desperate to decide to do that,' Kitty shared tautly. 'She went into labour before she arrived. She was dead by the time my grandparents reached the hospital. Grant wrote to them months afterwards asking if they'd had any news of her. They ignored the letter, but they kept it. The name and address of his solicitor was in it.' She hesitated, torn by his silence. 'I should have told you... I know I should have!'

'You do look like him,' Jake grated, swinging back to her. He loosed his breath in a hiss of anger. 'Do you know what I've gone through for eight years? And all this time... hell!' He thrust raking fingers through his wind-tousled hair. 'I'm talking off the top of my head. Put it down to shock. I have never wanted to hit anyone so badly, and the notion didn't leave me even when he said who he was. When I walked in here and found him...' He shook his head violently. 'But I was still going to take you home!'

'Were you?' she whispered.

'I missed you by hours in London. I don't think your father's housekeeper likes him very much.' A rueful quirk fleeted his lips. 'She invited me into the house, told me where you were and offered me the use of the phone. I received the distinct impression that she was hoping he was about to have his nose put out of joint.' The gleam of amused recollection evaporated and black lashes screened his gaze. 'Only I wasn't at all sure that I would have enough of a hold on you to do that.'

The pain roughly accentuating the stark admission tortured her. She twisted at the ribbon ties of her frothy *peignoir*. He took several restive steps away from her before he turned back. 'When I found you gone, I was shattered,' he muttered raggedly. 'Considering the way I behaved, you probably wonder why, but I didn't intend to drive you away. I wanted you to make a decision to put Maxwell and everything to do with him out of our lives, and if that meant shaming you into it, I was perfectly prepared to do it.'

Her eyes shimmered. 'I can understand that, but I think it's time that I told you what really happened to me...I mean, why I ended up with Grant,' she outlined shakily. 'My grandparents wrote to his solicitor and they sent me to him. He didn't get much choice about taking responsibility for me. You see, I never ran away. They told me to go and they told me not to come back...'

Jake's appraisal was intense, stark. 'Why?' he breathed. 'Why did they do that?'

Her eyes were pools of pain in her pale face. 'I lied to you, Jake. Don't you understand? I lied to you when I said I wasn't p...pregnant.'

Absolute silence greeted her confession. 'I didn't know what to do, I didn't know where to turn!' she sobbed

'I pretended it wasn't happening to me, and then of course I wasn't well and I couldn't hide it any longer.'

He captured her clenched hands and dragged her into his arms. 'Oh, dear God, why can't we turn the clock back?' he demanded unsteadily, muttering her name, smoothing her hair until his lean, hard strength calmed her and she clung to him. 'Why were you still protecting me, Kitty? You lied to me and I should have known you were lying. You were just a kid and you had to face that alone...' His roughened voice petered out as he crushed her against him.

'I never wanted anything as much as I wanted that baby,' she confessed in a surge of emotion. 'When I had the miscarriage, I wouldn't even believe the doctor when he said that it would have happened anyway. It made me so bitter.'

'I know... I know,' he whispered jerkily. 'You were expecting my child and I should have been there for you. I'll never forgive myself for that night.'

'But it wasn't your fault... it wasn't your fault,' she protested.

He drew in a long, shuddering breath. 'I was going to marry you as soon as I finished my training. I couldn't wait to get you out of that awful house. I had it all mapped out. I never once accepted that anything could go wrong. Naturally you were to be a virgin bride. I never once saw a future that didn't include you.'

'Don't,' she begged. 'I saw your mother. I know why, why you treated me like that.'

'It all came apart overnight,' he relived rawly. 'She killed it. Do you know why I believed her? Because we were so close. I didn't go to my father because I was afraid of what I might do. I couldn't believe that she would tell a lie like that about my father, not the way she felt about him. I didn't know how to keep myself away from you. That was the worst part of the nightmare and that's why I married Liz. With her around I thought I could still see you in the guise of a friend...'

She shivered, pierced by the savage bitterness powering those final words.

'Naturally the marriage was a disaster. You'd disappeared and I was half out of my mind with worry. When I found out the truth about you, I went off the deep end.' He was winding a shining strand of silver hair tightly round his fingers. 'If I'd lost you through something I'd done, I could have lived with it. But I couldn't live with it as it happened. I felt cheated. I never lied to Liz. I never pretended to love her, but she deserved a better deal than she got,' he completed grimly.

Kitty cleared her throat uncertainly. 'We were very young. It mightn't have worked for us either.'

'We had enough love to make it work,' he contradicted. 'I can't remember a time when I didn't love you. When you came back, I did genuinely intend to try and be a friend. Only I wasn't capable of that. I saw you again and that was it. Even though I couldn't get near you, even though I was eaten alive with jealousy, I could have laid my heart at your feet on the first day...'

'Why didn't you tell me what your mother had done?' she prompted frustratedly

His firm mouth compressed. 'At the beginning I thought I'd be making an ass of myself. You didn't want to know. And then that day at the Grange, I remembered how I'd felt that night and I'd have told you then.'

'I cut you off. I was scared,' she admitted.

'That makes two of us,' he confessed wryly. 'But when I got you to the church, I didn't believe that anything could ever come between us again.'

'And I let Grant come between us. I think I believed that, as long as you thought someone else might want me, you'd want me more. I was so terrified of losing you,' she confided half under her breath.

'Kitty.' It was an aching reproof. 'You never lost me. Never once in all these years. I didn't have any right to be jealous, but just the thought of you with another man turns me into a vicious bastard. I'll get over it. I'm not asking any questions.'

Her heart was in her damp eyes. 'There's never been another man, Jake. I've always loved you and I always will.'

He took her mouth in a passionately hungry assault, his hand roving to the ties on her filmy covering, jerking them loose to explore beneath. Her fingers tugged his shirt out of his jeans, her breath sobbing in her throat as she made contact with his warm, sensuous flesh.

With an inarticulate sound of frustration, he lifted his head. 'If you don't stop doing that, I won't be able to control myself long enough to explain why I lost my head over the Grange.'

'Stop doing what?'

He intercepted the hand roaming over the silk-smooth skin just below his waistband. 'You can take up exactly where you left off in a few minutes,' he promised unsteadily. 'Last winter on my thirtieth birthday I came into my grandmother's money. My father was a big disappointment to her, and before she died she cut him out of her will and made me her beneficiary. I was only a child and, since she had no idea how I would turn out, she ensured that I couldn't touch a penny before I was thirty.'

He had gained her attention. 'Your father must have been furious.'

Jake smiled ruefully. 'He tried to break the will but it was watertight. After his death, the bank would have foreclosed if it hadn't been for that inheritance waiting for me. But I couldn't force my mother and my sisters to live on the breadline for years. It wouldn't have been fair, so I sold up. However,' he paused, 'when the Grange fell empty, I began toying with the idea of offering to buy it back.'

In dismay she stared up at him.

'When I realised that you owned it, I blew a fuse. The thought that Maxwell's money had got there first was the final straw,' he acknowledged candidly. 'Have you any other surprises for me?'

'I have a Ferrari.'

Laughing, he swept her up and spread her like a captive slave on the bed. 'I can live with that. As long as I have you, I can live with anything.'

'A baby?' As he stilled halfway out of his shirt, she reddened. 'I was talking future possibilities.'

Hearing the defensive tone, he started to laugh again. 'Kitty, we have only been married for a few days.'

'I'm not very patient.'

'Now that you mention it,' he breathed huskily, 'neither am I.'

He engulfed her in a drugging kiss that sent her into a tailspin.

Jake wandered out of the bathroom, towelling dry his hair. 'Still in bed?' he mocked.

It was six in the evening. Kitty spread a complacent smile over her tall, beautifully proportioned husband and, when she could drag her eyes from him, over their spacious bedroom. They had moved into the Grange while the renovations were still in progress. An army of workmen had shared their home with them for months. Jessie was now presiding over the kitchen of her dreams and an adequate supply of daily helpers. Bob Creighton was still managing the estate, but Jake had superseded Colwell Holdings.

'Grant won't arrive before nine,' she whispered invitingly.

Jake came down on the bed beside her and stared down at her with amusement. 'Who's got the short straw?'

She stroked a persuasive finger gently across his cheekbone. 'I did it the last time.'

'And it was as if he'd been told there was a death in the family.'

She frowned. 'We could call this one after him . . . sort of sweeten the pill.'

Jake vented an appreciative laugh. 'Don't use that expression. He's highly likely to ask if we've ever heard of it. Beth is only six months old.'

'He did turn up at the christening,' she pointed out. 'I thought he'd chicken out last minute.'

'I have never seen anybody give a baby a wider berth.'

'We can tell him it's his fault. It was that Caribbean cruise on his yacht that did it,' she said seriously.

Jake covered her mouth hungrily. 'I was under the impression that I did it, and it doesn't take a change of climate to put me in the mood,' he muttered raggedly. 'How do you feel about celebrating again?'

In the end neither of them had to make the announcement. Tina did it for them over the dinner table. 'The doctor's giving my mummy another baby,' she relayed, proud as Punch as Grant almost choked on his wine.

Kitty's father cleared his throat. 'I think you ought to develop the stork story. It might be safer.'